WISDOM

Also by John Fraser
and published by
AESOP Modern Fiction:

Animal Tales
The Answer
Behaving Well
Best Friends
Black Masks
Blue Light / Starting Over
The Case
Confessions
Down from the Stars
The Ends of the Earth
Enterprising Women
The Future's Coming Everywhere
Happy Always
Hard Places
An Illusion of Sun
The Magnificent Wurlitzer
Medusa
Military Roads
The Observatory
The Other Shore
People You Will Never Meet
The Red Bird
The Red Tank
Runners
'S'
Short Lives
Sisters
Soft Landing
The Storm
Strangers and Refugees
Thinking Scientifically
Thirty Years
Three Beauties
Tomorrow the Victory
Wayfaring

WISDOM

John Fraser

AESOP Modern Fiction
Oxford

AESOP Modern Fiction
An imprint of AESOP Publications
Martin Noble Editorial / AESOP
28 Abberbury Road, Oxford OX4 4ES, UK
www.aesopbooks.com

First edition published by AESOP Publications

www.johnfraserfiction.com

A catalogue record of this book is
available from the British Library.

First edition 2021

ISBN: 978-1-910301-87-6

CONTENTS

STARDUST

All that I know of a certain star, Is ....
Mine has opened its soul to me, therefore I love it.

Robert Browning, *My Star*

IN THE MIDDLE of the ocean, our motor stopped. We stopped. The boat went to and fro, a silent roll and, we hope, no rock. The sea is all around and over us: the sky.

We're scientists. We know what happens next. And after.

'Man is what he eats,' Pietro says to me, and grins. 'So if I eat you, I'll have your wisdom – and your fear.'

The last one left will be a sage. It will take years to wear us down – the ballast is all lemon rice. A precaution for expeditions – it makes sense. We shall eat, and go higher till we scarcely touch the waves, and scud....

Our belts won't go round our plimsoll lines.

Then we heard of the catastrophe on land. Disaster for everyone but us.

We are unknown, our catastrophe belongs to us alone.

The sea – our mission was to search the coasts: the sea's indifferent, I suspect it must despise the cliffs and beaches: or ignore, reject them. Land – its antithesis and challenge.

'It's serious,' the captain, Adil, says. 'No one knows we're here. The "here" is not of import to us, we're stranded, but it would signify greatly to a rescuer.'

'And are we stranded?' Pietro asks. 'We came to look for strands – but now we're free, we're landless, ocean proletarians; we wander, wind-destined, to and fro ... like hungry gulls.'

'I suspect old Mister Noah,' Doctor Chin chimes in, 'remembered when there was all sea, no land. The flood would have brought back memories – of being birthed in tempests, mermen with fins, in swarms, pods: in shoals.... The birds came later, naturally; for fishmen, there'd be no one they must dodge, nothing with wings, at least....'

Adil's impatient. 'Everyone,' he says, 'must categorise himself. By gender and by preference: we're all scientists, so there is no preference. We have the same rules, beliefs, procedures, set the same standard – so ... there is no gender. But you,' he points at me, 'you, Hadar – you're an observer. You write it up, what happens to us. So, you must outlive us all ... and not intrude. Your doings don't come in – nor who you are, or where you've been. Observe our destinies. Pretend you are a scientist, pretend you are what you are not. Write. Don't "be". If we are rescued, we must know exactly who is who ... Though why should we concern ourselves? It's for the history. It signifies, but not right now. So, tell: what shall we enter as your category?'

'I hate the sea,' I say. 'I don't like you, not anyone, not any one of you. Except – there's Doctor Chin. If earth is left, I hope the Doctor will inherit it.'

The others press around – I'm categorised. A sceptic, ignorant, and maybe magical in my thought, my cosmology. But I accept: have your way with naming me. If there's to be cannibalism, I need friends.

'This is a prison hulk,' the captain says. 'So bonding's natural – like jealousy and sex.'

'Perhaps you're angling for another berth, Hadar,' says Pietro. 'Another, smaller boat. To do your observations in. Treachery, my friend.'

'We're not the objects,' Adil says. 'Of anything; research, experiment, hypothesis. But – what are we now? We're subjects without objects. What is our field? There is no matter but ourselves, the boat.... The rest is liquid nights. And we are lost. What is outside us, as we drift? What is our context, how does the water understand us, as we toss...? The sea's our scientist. It will find us, inspect – and then?'

'There's fish to classify,' Pietro says. 'But we shall eat all that we've angled for. They will be us. Shall we be them?'

'Easy,' says Doctor Chin. 'We came to study waves and coasts. There are no coasts, so we are free! In science, freedom is an indeterminacy. That's what we're in, and are – and Hadar too.'

'Hadar doesn't fit,' says Adil. 'Does that matter? Which of us can steer by the stars? That's what they call it, but they mean "steer and move accordingly in some direction...."'

'They left that out at school,' says Pietro. 'Stars knowing where we are. Like the zodiac. Knowing what we'll be. Now, we're in a horrorscope –' and he laughs. 'We can voyage with the moon – it takes us far far away, and fast – if only ... we could hitch a tow ... harness a tide....'

*

Coastal erosion – that was our mission. The sea's appetite – to take it all, in nibbles and gulps. Who's side are you on?

*

'Everyone must have a project,' Adil says. 'Hadar – it's settled: you'll observe ... us; with objectivity. You need a distance, I suppose. If a small abandoned boat drifts by – it's yours. That is the writer's badge, transport, conveyance, diligence.... Solitude requires a coracle.... Write down the lot: your life; experience. The women and the men.... How you are qualified....'

'That's super naff,' says Doctor Chin. 'It's like at school – what you did on holidays. A chore. A bore.'

Women on board – don't want to be categorised as such. They're right – Adil has over-reached.

'This is a spot,' says Adil. 'We're in, and on. There is no specific time, no seconds and no history. We don't know where we are on sea, or earth. We're scientists, so we don't have, need, characters. That should help Hadar with his work. A streamlined fiction. We're marooned. He must not be becalmed! He'll be in absolute control, a super-modernist.'

'That's imagining,' says Doctor Chin. 'Imagination is much over-estimated. We all have one, it's ungovernable –

full of viral stuff, like fear, anxiety and dread. You're advised not to license it, or train or trammel it. Let it roam! But there is nowhere that it can. Imagination – is a can of peeled tomatoes! Better pick the real thing....'

'Doctor Chin!' I say. 'You worry at meaning like a cat and mouse.'

'And which am I?' asks Doctor Chin. 'You'd best be both. It's science. Consider: if I say to you, Hadar, "I imagine that I love you, that this voyage has been an imaginary epic of unfathomed eros and its psyche," I expect you'd be quite miffed, and disappointed. You'd start again believing in reality, and hoping I would stop you being cast as castaway....'

We hug tight in our bunk. 'Oilskins ...' says Doctor Chin, dreamily. 'That's what we sailors wear. That's what we sailors have.'

'We're not wearing anything,' I say.

'You've missed the point again,' says Doctor Chin.

*

'If you scan the chart,' says Adil, 'you'll note these latitudes are home to sea monsters of appalling size. Of course, the admiralty's a scaredy bunch that loves to fantasise in charts. But we must keep a lookout – many seamen's tales involve a swallowing, regurgitation, that may lie ahead. We're drifting down the earth's curve. It is gravity. Usually our friend, it draws us down ... the cold ... the lockdown in the ice.... We cannot walk to land – there is catastrophe abroad.... Ours is unknown except to us – theirs, maybe a mystery to everyone.'

*

The stars – like snowflakes ... no, they don't twinkle, not at all. It's cold air that makes it seem that way....

*

Be very careful, Hadar,' says Doctor Chin. 'Professor Hoover – he of leisure studies – he believes you are a fraud. When times were good, he had no style, and no endurance. He would like the boat to drift down south – the land of ice, and drop you there. Try to avoid him – he'll not be convinced ... he's after you....'

The stars – a mat of them, as if a clumsy printer dropped a tray of cleaned full-stops on the floor.... Behind the brighter ones, the paler, smaller ones – behind those....

No – for sure, they don't give directions, don't signal down to newspapers the destiny of each of us next day....

'It's horrible,' I say to Doctor Chin. 'Each time it happens: a catastrophe. Regrets, the anguish ... death, the waltzing vinctrix, takes us in her arms and wafts us to the deep....'

'If they put you off,' says Doctor Chin, 'on ice or boat – I'll be so sorry for you – but a guy like you, observing, writing down your thoughts – it's all imagination. Here – nothing happens, nothing at all. No need for your imaginings. Time pries out our bones. It's quiet, indifferent, the lemon rice goes rancid.... Hadar, this is peace. Eternal. Silent.'

Dear Doctor Chin. I ask, 'Suppose I tell my life – there's women there ... I shall not clothe them, love them, but you'll guess. Don't react. No jealousy! I reminisce – the bocks on lime-tree avenues, the gardens, Luxembourg and Isfahan, hot nights in Sfax – time lost, and not again discovered, not remembered, all the characters fused and melted, all entwined like jelly-babies in a box left on the radiator....'

'Put in some jokes,' says Doctor Chin. 'They make time – lost, found or misremembered – pass more pleasantly....'

*

We muster on the foredeck. Many many profs and tars. I put my arm round Doctor Chin. The sea humps and holes like couples restless under covers – 'It's always fascinated me,' I say. 'The force! It could be a resource for us – no hurt, no damage, and no cost.... It's there – useless, a palace, grounds with fountains, made by no one for the cods and sprats....'

'Hush,' says Doctor Chin, and laughs. 'They know all that, the whitecoats here. That is their job! The sea is eating up our land: they're here to change its appetite, and have it run our TVs and our bedside lamps....'

'I'd heard about this, Doctor Chin,' I say, embarrassed. 'There's many ways we've tried to make that work ... like building suns and stars. This is groundswell. I've seen fusion ... forever anticipated, coming round the bend ... Power, Chin: energy....'

They'd like to drop me off – I'm the unwelcome chronicler, the truth expert, the limner of their enterprise – maybe the bad augur of our plight.

*

Before they can find us, they must find we're lost.

*

Here's what I told to Doctor Chin. What I had done. How I had the need to ship out here....

*

'You worked with Tokamak – building the smallest of the stars. There's so many up there, down there. Quite avuncular – they twinkle! You didn't get anywhere, though?'

The casual guy interviewing me tries to look on top. He dresses offhand, so you feel he couldn't care if you get the job and work alongside him for ever. Or not. Never see you again.

It was a failure, the Tokamak.

And they thought I brought bad luck.

Wherever else I went and tried – someone tried – to build a star, it failed. It would be making us immortal, proving our species was the one meant to survive. No chance.

Each species at its summit faces a final test to seal its dominance. Don't fail!

They dropped a bomb on dinosaurs. Too bad for them!

We've used up everything: it's hot. It's cold. It's arid. I don't dwell on failure, on mere non-success. The same thing, of course; but if you fail the final exam – you're still around, a little tattered.

It was much worse, more complicated, with our star that wasn't born.

It was like making a swimming-pool out of twine.

I say, 'I took it as a judgement. All the other stars were there, from many years ago. We couldn't do it, not even a little one in a box. Something else had made millions of them ... a production line of immense antiquity and proportions.

'Fusion should be possible, but there is uncertainty, the plasma is like gooseberry jelly, it roams about and wobbles. It's as volatile as plankton or the clingy stuff that ghosts emit ... ectoplasm.... That's the stuff we're dealing with. Mediums have it in their bag: a super-plasma. You'd think, with all the ghosts around, there'd be a big supply. Indeed there is – but it's capricious, moody. Now you don't see it ... now you do. Now the shades start seeking justice....'

Is the uncertainty due to us, our test, our project? Or is it a trick built in to the design? Who by? Other grandiose ideas – like Soviet man ... they failed....

Or maybe it's a caprice of all the ghosts still in the cellars and the camps – far from home and their identity?

It's about hot water and electric toothbrushes, isn't it? My star....

Or is it about who runs the new motor that powers the world? Who's aspiring to be the topmost monster...? That's slippery too!

As the Duce found, you can't be Duce without the people, but the people will be the people without the Duce.

So what?

So what should happen now? What's to be done? Where do we go? Poetry? Or gardening?'

*

He says, 'I see it isn't science bothers you – it's ghosts.'

*

I have been honest – a mistake. I make a poor impression. Truth fills, defiles, every place and every continent, like a toxic fart.

'You could give me a trial,' I say.

We who feel guilty always seek a trial – hoping for a pardon, not a punishment.

The boss in the interview – he wants a hand, not a puzzle.

*

'I'm of a higher class than you,' says my lover, Alcine. 'This chattering about a job ... if you were anyone, you'd have enough money, friends – to let you talk of other things....'

'Class is not a high or low,' I say. 'It's what it does – control or bolstering, steering, deciding. Or else you pay for being low-born with your life: working, submitting.

'What you mean is culture. You're higher up the mound. Social groups are distinguished by their practices – your family has the cash, the ideology, the push that gives you airs, because you fancy you are bosses. You worship differently; read books, hear music, gaze at pictures, clouds, flowers, and animals, in your own way. But you're bugs like all the rest. Too bad for you. I run if I see a cop. You primitives salivate when you hear the dinner bell.... You're crass. Like me. The real upper crust's a connoisseur of carillons.

'But when our civilisation falls down, you'll have been bombed. The gods desert. You'll go to jail ... or worse.'

'It happens to everybody, dear,' she says. 'Whether you're a boss or slave. People are foreigners to each other, whatever their position. They act by instinct – like colonists and colonized.... Some drill, so others fight.'

MINA

A name quite like that; a city, must be on the map, but if you look it up, it isn't there.

Everybody went into the star. Worked on its absence. A black cast-iron boiler, a mine that ought to float. Every morning, everybody, into the cauldron, lilting in, like the children into the mountain. The mountain – might it just have thrust up, exploded? – the rock holding the heat of earth and sun. Blank faces, minds – hallucinating? As if the shift awoke, ate a platter of peyote porridge, and filed into its imagination.

The star. Dense; engulfing matter, spilling it out. Still cold, leaking.

Outside: we – I – wandered. Death: as you imagined. Regretful, sometimes you wept ... this, the world before you entered it, before anyone at all was there ... the houses, rivers, clouds and foxes – all set up, a director's cut all ready; prepared and painted for your scenes. Too lifelike even. Living, ticking over – but you, like all the others who're not here, not visible at all, not ever, not to anyone, those who don't exist – dead. All as it should be. Just – no people. None of their sounds. Even cars, parked and licensed – no drivers, none, not ever, no past, no one to come and turn the key and be the no one going nowhere. A new wing of paradise, just opened and not populated. No judgement, no god, no angels but birds ... modest and routine – the cries a black, gold, cerise splash, a randoming tessera on the blue.

You. Me. The only one in this sooty bubbling universe ... hallucinating nicely. Like all the places left deserted – the world all over an immense mistake. A rough cut, a huge sketch abandoned, every detail ... just – unused, unwanted.

The star – wingless. Made to stay down here. Quite inconceivable, its making and its destiny.

*

Building a sun, when you have no resources, it's your hope, the species' straw. When it fails, there's just the cycle of illnesses, the waiting for your turn. The hunted hare in the bare field. Each targeted animal succumbs to fear and lead: the first word learned – the end. The runts go first, and then the older wiser ones.... Building our sun, our star – it was a fantasy, but all there was.

*

Alcine's heard it before.

'I was an observer,' I say. 'They wouldn't let me in. I saw nothing – so, no need to be expelled. I hadn't lost my innocence, nor felt the heat, the heat of our own sun to come, one day, soon.

'The workers – every morning – they went in, they failed – and home to bed. The next day.... Follow orders, failure. Home. Work. They were without sin....'

'Without success too,' says Alcine.

'I was a zombie. I didn't speak the language well, people thought I was a spy, dangerous, somehow.

'But – I had a cat,' I say. 'I loved it, and it loved me, and then I went away and left it.... How I miss that cat....'

*

'I hallucinated. I walked on my age, my years: high tottering heels – my mortality, of course – like I was walking in an actor's boots, *cothurni* – I might totter, fall, and go on falling ... the answer to mortality – it must be immortality ... and yet – the universe goes on, it seems for ever, but it's insidious. Not friendly, not straight, not straight and forward: – full of gas ... empty of – everything except for gravity? It pulls me down – even my immortality....'

I must voyage, among the strange things ... the forces. The pits and whirligigs, the voids, the whirlpools, the sucking dark....

She breaks in – 'It wouldn't have been a proper star. Not that you could wish on, guide your galleon. Just a buzzing power-station.... Like the French one, Iter, that doesn't quite exist.'

The people who don't speak to me, those don't exist, or who exist, but somewhere else. If I'm an alien, what do I ask about? The blackflies? The camps? Some guilt somewhere? A death sentence – was it earned by me, who wasn't then alive? A crime against the non-existent people here – who weren't even thought of? ...

Where did socialism go?

And they ask back, 'You want sustenance? Which of us is strange? You or us?'

The starmen. If they climb down the ladders, down from the stars – will they ask 'You want immortality, and yet you eat those living, beautiful things. Why don't you eat each other? Humane abattoirs for humans? Hook up your philosopher, hang him in the chimney, smoke him like a turkey....'

But they don't ask, don't suggest. They're heavenly bodies, our angels who never asked, and if they spoke, it wasn't useful; not an equation, not a pulse, a wave. No explanation, not of anything.

*

'Those are places you write about, to give you courage, walk off your stress. But when you're in them and can't leave,' she says. 'You can't account for your unease.'

'I would have stayed,' I say, 'but they'd reached a billion degrees. Nearly the right road ... I wanted them to have a victory, a little one. First – a star, a sun. Then, perhaps – a black hole? A fraction of the celestial parade, of course. You don't see God at once. Nor the devil: that one you carry with you in your pedlar's pack.

'It is the force you seek, not to harness, but to create from nothing: repetitive, and formulaic, making emptiness and uninhabitability, useless, crazy, inhuman and irrational. But what imagination! What an exposure of our tales, our liminal, our sub-unconscious.... Revelation, Alcine – that's what there should have been, not engineering.'

'You make it sound a TV series. Cheering on the fantasy. Special effects and bad acting,' she says. 'And you observed. Nothing happened, so you couldn't write it up.'

'If you want a revelation, even if it doesn't come, it must give you inspiration,' I say. 'Like – I could have had a kinder life. Been less cool.'

*

I searched everywhere for that Russian reactor – not on the ground: on paper, on the ether. I never found a trace of it – like those old Soviet cities, it was out of bounds, not on local maps. But the satellites could have seen, and they could report nothing. The people who planned it? search! Up comes: 'this article has been cancelled' ... 'biography is private'... 'you are not authorised' , 'nothing'. Stop looking.

I can't go and see – just now, we can't go anywhere.

*

'It's strange, Alcine,' I say. 'The need to feel someone else's skin, their flesh – it can make you love them. Without that – you're a poor wandering soul. A beast in the forest looking for another ... a coupling.'

'It doesn't bother me at all,' says Alcine, 'not being that other person, not of that species, not of yours, not wanting to follow you in the search for things that don't exist, or are closed off from you. It's only convention that drives you. If you find forbidden things – it's just a reference, a headnote. You can't love a thought. The more you want – the person, other persons, a world, society – it's not there, ephemeral. Second bests, illustrations – the more you'll want, the less you find. It's logical.'

She kisses me and moves away.

*

'They failed, Alcine,' I say, despairing. 'It's not just an experiment. If it works, it's the end of your world, and of you in your world. If it fails – the same.

'Every experience is "future-oriented". That's a true saying. It makes you think of where you've been, where your fear is taking you.... When we look up at the sun, our sun, and feel its heat, its warmth – we think "if you're not there?" Are you our enemy, our fate at least: our destiny?'

Alcine turns away: 'The certainty of uncertainty is only part of it,' I go on. 'It's my training. Science and society. My life's spent with one foot in each. I'm entering my own head....'

'I'm not laughing,' she says. 'But you're funny. Everlastingly funny.'

'We couldn't solve the puzzle. It's not the end. The end is plague. All the Pilgrims thought of, was sex,' I say. 'Like in the Decameron. It concentrates the mind on matter, you search for it, in the ganglia, the memories, the concepts ... for something material, that receives, that thrusts, that extends and welcomes. People, Alcine, thought your thoughts, bodies made your body – and if it ends, where does it end, where does it *go?* Everything ends, but nothing, nothing at all, disappears; it's all on the inventory, a ranch-brand on the membrane, a tessera cemented to a cloud....'

Nothing to say to that. How I want her, Alcine: and how I wish she were not Alcine.

'This torment,' she says, 'you invent it all. We go on, adjust. You will too, but in misery ...'

'Yes,' I say. 'I could have had a better life. Much better, with no need to talk about it.... Now – I'm always ahead of you – looking back on what you tell me about myself, as if I know how it will turn out, how it will seem – all in a little time.

'You tell me, "you're looking fit," and it is so. But me – I'm looking back. Yes, that's how I seemed then, but now I know how it will all turn out.'

'It's a common feature. You imagine you are dead, and looking back,' she says. 'You must be sad: depressed. But you were talking about magnetism, about fusion – the big slow test.'

She's analysing what I say, up with me, shoulder to shoulder. But I'm future. She's in the now, the present.

'It can't be done,' I say. 'Making a sun, and keeping it in a pot. It sounds easy. It could be done. But always we're too late. Something else – always cropping up. And anyway – not a star, a sun, to warm you, light you up: – just a black kettle.'

*

'You and Alcine,' says Bonnie, 'it was heavy. But not going anywhere. People tire of the big names you've dropped, and you're not bright, just obsessive. Hints, evasions.'

'What did we hope to have, Bonnie?' I ask: 'Voltaire would have loved it – a French sun, that never illuminated.

'One morning I had a dream – varied landscapes, losing my clothes in bars, bars dark, deserted – everybody gone somewhere I should be making for – but I stayed, and gradually the places opened up, lights, girls in sequins served me booze, and slid away when I got talking. Somewhere – I acquired this big metal and plastic frame – like American football posts, but a totem, a ritual object, with bells and white embellishments – an 'H' basically, that I had to lug around, and carry up the stairs to ... people like they are in wonderland ... not quite animals, not quite not. Full of advice – if only I could stand up straight and not sway and judder.... There was a prostitute....'

'And you chatted, and she was mature, a motherly type, and you were too pissed to go with her....' says Bonnie, looking bored, amused.

'It ended well,' I say. 'I kept the frame, was all set to carry it along the country road, all overshadowed with thick willow trees and beyond there was a river, maybe a lake....'

'I hear that all the time,' says Bonnie. 'People go on cruises to see bears – then they come back and tell a stupid dream to me. It's all they could remember of the trip.'

'The totem, the talisman,' I say. 'That was original.'

'So was Tokamak,' she says. 'I like you, but we shan't be together very long.'

'I'm sorry about that,' I say. 'Very sorry.'

'The dream – it's your purgatory,' she says. 'You're doing well in it. Most of us are. Those who can't cope – they'll not be missed.'

'In the old days,' I say. 'A philosopher would love it if he got a wrong answer to some question. It would open up another track. But – failed science... What does that mean, what does that signify? A dead end. Maybe with good intentions. But wrong... Useless. Almost useless, anyway.'

'Leave them,' Bonnie says. 'Leave the stars where they are. Be good to the sun. That's the answer. But the answer doesn't count for much. It's odd.... There's so much you want from a question, different things. One answer that could mean everything has an answer. When we ask, "Can I make a star?" – who are we asking? Maybe we know much more always than we say ... so we've given up: it's not really a question....'

*

We're going to the fairground. A cop stops us: 'Go home!' he says.

We don't cohabit. Don't have 'a home'.

We'll sort his order out.

Is it a locust storm? An escape of gas? of prisoners?

We're not quite sure – there's what we hear and what we know – far far apart. We're imprisoned – jailed in our home, imprisoned in our family, if one is to hand.

What I did before this, is a mystery. It's all changed ... where did I hide? Who did I speak to on the street? What did I read?... Who did I think I was? In your room, confined, you've lost your personality, all you want is out. 'Out' gives you your shape, a name. The indoors is as it always was, the outdoors is a movie ... It's like the ghetto, a ghetto customised for one. An endless sentence. Who's the Director? The Dictator? Who can we trust? Will they come to save us? Or bombard....? What did we do?

*

Everybody knew it would happen.

*

Whatever it is, it can't be stopped. It's part of our failure, like with Tokamak.

I always thought – reality is metaphysical. It can be anything, transformed, unexplained. Or like taffy – to be twisted, swallowed.

I could have had a happy life – a happier life. Avoided the boredom – France, Russia, the waiting.

Revolutions popping off like puffed wheat.

I spent too long watching other people not doing what they couldn't, and doing nothing myself, except watching – not even with a good style, with perfect orthography. My career – deadlines – dead lines.

*

Alcine – I never knew much about her – she wanted to tell her story. How she'd struggled. And disappeared.

I could call Bonnie, but like Alcine, she isn't there, gone. To work in psychology you must have a mind and believe in it.

It's a revelation, that she could call me, speak on the phone! If she wanted.

*

'All over!' Bonnie says. 'Normal again. Like before, only now, being very very careful.'

*

'And so,' says Doctor Chin, 'that's why you're here. Curiosity. Your tale might seem depressing – but we searchers recognise it as a dare. All lives end, but no life finishes – the regret you feel is not for what you've lost, but for what you have not found.'

'No,' I say. 'It isn't so. Not for you. They'll rescue you, you'll hurry on, you'll get the cash because you say you'll save the species, but in fact – your landscape is sublime indifference; the virtual infinity, inscrutability, of everything – matter, anti-matter, void and motion, the space, the energy, the distance and uncertainty, the wastes, the hecatombs of everything that lives and creeps and clings to life, is eaten, starved, decays.... There's no humanity, dear Doctor, in where you go and what you do: that, the universe: *that* is the horror ... the insentient cold, the consuming everlasting heat.... Apparent emptiness; instead, that's full of useless stuff....'

'I'm right, you're wrong, Hadar,' says Doctor Chin, quite brisk. 'Now, there's a sing-song – Professor Hoover is a wiz at Hahn. You should hear his "*Mon rêve était d'avoir un amant*...." We all cry. You, though – watch out. The danger grows.'

Doctor Chin won't hold my hand. 'I'm valuable,' says Doctor Chin. 'They'll rescue me – a plank, canoe – an iceberg....'

'But,' I say, 'you are invisible! Not to me – but to the world....'

'We mostly deal with stuff like that,' says Doctor Chin. 'Invisibles – except on our notebooks. Imagine – you are Endymion – the moon will sleep with you, and then it's off! I'm off! Voyaging....'

'You're stuck here like the rest, my love,' I say.

'You've missed the point,' says Doctor Chin.

Fusion never has quite worked. Doctor Chin's experiment, being rescued, leaving us here? – another failed experiment, like teletransportation.

'Oh, Hadar,' says Pietro, who's white with anguish and annoyance, 'Us guys do lots of experiments, and almost each one fails. That is the point. But the last one's always called successful....'

'That's Jesuitry, Pietro,' I say. 'This time travel – much too complicated. Incantations – they're like hope – they usually don't work. Tokamak – it's a spell, a key without a door. A door....'

'Yes, yes,' he says, irritated. 'But if Doctor Chin is rescued, it won't change the world, the universe. Nothing does. It changes by itself. Just trace the rules, and ... the exception is the rule, once you discover it. The rule was always there, and so there's no exceptions. Just you finding out more rules. Don't forget – the spell is an equation nobody forgets. And Doctor Chin – a humble-looking soul, in reality a high flier....'

Instinctively, I look up. There's the sailor's star, there's Saturn. Isn't Kronos up there too?

Doctor Chin, whatever the means, has disappeared, while we have our faces tilted up.

No trace!

I feel I've sloughed a skin.... Nature moving on....

'The Doctor has no sin,' says Adil, using a telescope to scope out – nothing. 'No links with dirty demons. Science – knowing the right trick for the right trick – the vanishing boy – up the rope, never comes down; and get it wrong and he's dismembered, the body parts rain on your audience ... you're in deep shit....'

The sea – grey-blue humps ... Where do they go? To shores, like sailors? And there, what do they do? Like sailors?

*

Doctor Chin had said, 'It's an illusion. Almost all the sea is motionless. It doesn't travel, just a fringe turns white like savants' hair, then is exhausted, flops down on the sand. The rest is waiting for me, my summons, my bridle and my bit – an immense mass ... the power!'

'If it's supine, Doctor Chin,' I said. 'Where's the energy?'

'Oh, it's there,' said Doctor Chin. 'You need the word to wake it up. And the word's not Tokamak!'

A burst of laughter! What fun!

*

As for Doctor Chin – the escape? Can it repeat, be mine? Too soon to say. You must hypothesise, but that approach – is old-time philosophy; reality's not yes or no, or now and nevermore, and, still less, right or wrong.

'I want more than this, Pietro,' I say. 'More, or less. I must anyway stick to my genre. Doctor Chin's a genius – a national asset. Maybe they sent a submarine.... These big countries – they keep a track on where the fish go; sharks and whales. And dolphins too. The good Doctor may have had a way to talk to them .. to everyone. To bosses....

'I want – not wisdom, not something unserviceable, painfully acquired, but to see how it all links up. How it might all – all that happens – have connections, even if it's just for me .... Doctor Chin said my emotions were too slippery – like fish in water, like water round a fish.... These people, fish, professors – how do they fit in? They peer at me, goggle, then drift on ... There must be simple answers.... Do emotions make it all go round? I'm sceptical....'

'There is a very simple clue,' says Pietro. 'It started with a bang. An explosion: no meaning, no purpose, and no order. Blast patterns we call rules. We're pilgrims, Hadar, slogging our way through devastation to a shrine no one has ever reached. Because there isn't one.'

'The experts,' I say. 'They throw us together, you and I – and we're not compatible. We don't like each other. Are we Hoover's experiment in incompatibility? And – surely, they'd have thought of some breakdown, foreseen the need for an evacuation.... Making the ballast edible – it shows foresight....'

'It's the plague,' says Pietro. 'That's the breakdown. When it's in the streets and you're shut in, you're sick, infected, whether or not you itch and sweat.... The rice – it's made us all delirious. They don't do funerals, but the more we eat, the more space there's made for our cadavers in the holds.'

'We did bad, of course,' I reflect. 'But mostly we aren't punished. The wars we started. Wars we didn't stop. Famines ... the rest. Nature. Our self-destructiveness.'

'There's inflatables,' says Pietro. 'You're an observer. I'm nothing much, and young: we are their ravens. They'll send us two out to look for land. When we're far off and can't get back – they'll know they must drift on, and send the doves. The doves find land. Then it's a story once again.

'There's measurements and diving – like your Doctor Chin does, like a silvery fish ... but we two, we're not assets, we're just part of their plan.'

'This sea stuff,' I say. 'It sickens me. Somehow, it's underhand. Treachery beneath the rolling slick. The star, that was magnificent.... My star, the one that wasn't cooked.'

I keen: *woe, woe Russia....*

'That's poetry,' says Pietro. 'Though, to reach a star you'd need become ancient – two hundred years at least it takes. And it's not stars you'd want to find – it's planets, they are grey and cold, or grey and hot. What would you eat there?

You'd be stuck, stuck for your next two hundred years – always hungry!' and he laughs.

'These catastrophes,' I say, appalled at the thought of a useless boat trip with Pietro as chief matelot. Would he eat me, if we run out of gas?.... 'Plague was celebrated as a test of character, bringing out varying psychologies; reflections on significance.' ... Now, it's different. These guys seem to have a plan, they're testing the weak links, me especially, to see if I react....

'It's not just you,' says Pietro in a huff: 'And, you're scared of Professor Hoover, I am scared of everyone. Especially you. You're brittle. Cranky. Crazy.'

*

They cast us off. We have no food. Hoover's delighted – 'Go boys! seek! Fetch! Find land, bring some back.'

He has no faith....

Drifting. The smell of rubber, and of Pietro, sicking up his everything.

There's a long spit of sand in the distance. No people. A good sign.

'The guys on the boat were wrong,' I say. 'Except, if we wanted, we couldn't tell them.'

'Wrong? You're simplistic,' Pietro says. 'One of the many reasons why I dislike you. They don't know what wrong is.'

THE SINGULARITY OF VENUS

'The morning and the evening star are one,' I say. 'Making a study, we can find out where we are. You must assist, Pietro. As a sailor, as a scholar – it's your strongest point – observe, like me....'

'Not so,' he says. 'We must build two huts, so we two don't collide. I've always been a wastrel, Hadar, a joker, spoiler. Critical critic, you might say. Then, having found us shelter – what do we eat?'

'I had in mind a brusque communiqué,' I say, 'to tell Professor Hoover and the rest, "We found the land, and we know where we are." If we want, we'll study our more distant part: we'll map the stars ... It's where all culture starts....'

'Oh no,' Pietro says, 'The culture starts right where you wear your pants. That is our problem – not the stars....'

So, the horror of our coexistence starts....

The food is easy – there's abandoned stores – an empty hypermarket, stuck and deserted, like Crusoe's galleon. People run – it's normal. Too bad – Crusoe's big ship, try not to go below – the rows of shackled slaves, underwater, dancing so slow, slow-slow-slow, no smile, the whole ship moves – maybe the whales give out a beat.... Hundreds of them – great dismasted ships beneath the sea.

Most civilisations started so: gorging, as we do, on what earlier ones have left. The problem of where to start – that's easily resolved. For Pietro, the next culture's in his groin. For me, watch the starry heavens – they fix our place, our distances, our regularities.... Order. Not guessing, not hypotheses – the rhythm, knowing our location, sighting our building....

'I'm not a Jungian, Pietro,' I tell him, to forestall polemics. 'But I'm more Jung than Freud. Lie on the sand, forget your animality, and watch the constellations....'

'You're back to front, Hadar,' he says. 'You've seen them try to make a star. *Nada.* We ate the world and threw the rind on to the fire. Live with your failure, accept the limitations.... It's useless, irritating too, to see you go back and try again. Or even worse, watch someone else make the attempt. You've not the means, still less the brain.... We're simple souls. Someone will find us, we'll be chivvied and forgotten. Maybe put in jail for being without documents and explanations....'

'Did they plan it all, Pietro? Those on the ship, masters of the watery world, the deep and dark?' I ask.

'Oh, there were factions there,' he says wisely. 'Fishmen and oceanmen, waves and depths ... but those were little plots inside a bigger one.'

'Getting rid of us?' I ask. 'I tell the truth, report a failure – that's enough, I guess. But you were thick with Adil, Professor Hoover too.'

He shows me his bio, tacked to his shack: 'Harvard Business. 90 kg. Wall Street Knuckle Club, Trader'.

'I knew more than anyone,' he says. 'It's all a fraud. Adil did naval studies – learned to steer – not start the engine, though. I – signed on as an accountant ... had to get away ... debts propel you better than the gasoline.'

I can't put up a similar bravure. I stare at him. 'Ah! Tokamak,' he says. 'I had a bet on that.'

'Would you have eaten me, Pietro?' I ask – it's my big concern, it seems.

'It bothers you, I see:' he says. 'If you're caught hungry – drink the blood and dry the flesh. That's what you do – it's economics.'

'Just one question, Pietro,' I say. 'Are we the subjects of an experiment?'

'They observe,' he says. 'Those guys on the boat, becalmed: they are the hundred eyes of God. But unlike you, Hadar, failure won't come in their minds. You want definitive results. They always have results: but solutions? Very rare. Yes, maybe we are an experiment – something marginal.

'You want the truth, Hadar, and assurance that our species is a worthy one. That's so far too much, it's dangerous.

'I want a truth recognised as well. That chaos follows chaos, problems are created, there are massacres, or something's bodged. The ignorant take power, and improvise, or harvest hecatombs.. And on and on, crisis to crisis, heroes infinite and humble. You think there might be resolutions, Hadar, but you fear there will not be. You're right to feel the chill, to feel depressed.

'I know how ignorance and superstition rule the world; the whitecoats are its handmaidens, its doctor-jailers. The systems work like that. I've been on the trading floor. There, we sell souls – alive, or dead – or moribund.

'What piques your curiosity, Hadar? The secrets of the sea, the stars? A detail. Banal, old hat, never enough. Like a can of kerosene to start an engine....'

*

Small waves break on the sand. I think of Doctor Chin: the waves break over my feet. A touch of pathos. I weep.

*

'It's what we were made for,' Pietro says. 'Primitives.'

'There are no primitives,' I say. 'Different modalities of thought, scales of knowledge, of verifications. Nothing is primitive, only there are different civilizations....'

'Don't fool yourself,' says Pietro. 'We're not a civilisation. And we think primitive.'

'Crusoe had a culture – he didn't bother much about his Friday,' I say. 'A handmedown was good enough for him.'

'They shoulda had kids,' says Pietro. 'Those know nothing.'

We leave it there.

*

'Maybe you've thought,' Pietro says, quite mischievous. 'When we two had gone – they all dived overboard. They'd want to turn the evolution back, become amphibious, or even stay down there. Make weapons, farm, do massacres ... just like it was up here.'

'I've thought of that,' I say. 'I even wrote a piece. The trouble is that in the end, it all starts off again. You waddle up the beach and see the stars – and don't go down again.

Philosophy has never thought too much of it, forgetting everything, recommencing as a fish or bird....'

'It would explain,' Pietro persists. 'Why they didn't want an accountant, an observer, who watch them go down off the side. And you're wrong. It's not forgetting anything. You've flown. You've watched TV – the camps, all that. Up, down, you've seen it all, experienced everything – even coral reefs. You don't forget, and yet you can go back to what you were before.

'You, Hadar, may have set store in writing down your memories – but everybody else tucks the info in their brains. Unused, unusable – it's there. When you hear the menace, the whooping and the feet in panic or in two-four time – you know exactly what to do. And that it doesn't work.'

'Do you surmise, Pietro?' I ask: maybe the idiot has a point..... 'Or do you know that's what they went to do? All in black, like newts, over the side and joyful?'

He looks at me. He doesn't say.

*

We'll never know.

*

Emotions. They're always with us. You can't be without one, or many. If you don't have one, you're certainly dead. But when we describe them – they're labels on empty bottles. Or inscriptions on a spate. Every language has its own set, that aren't yours ... maybe foreigners feel it different, everything?

And – some are really behaviours, or conditions – *joie, gaité, bonheur.* Stage directions.

Sadness. Very sad. 'Very sorry to hear....' Hearing is inevitable anyway. Regret ...nostalgia. A void to fill an emptiness. Glad – glad tidings – you can't use that now ... it's tinsel; and most are plastic – they don't dissolve, but you ought not use them: tears, laughter. Gone with the breeze. Bringing moisture from your well and spilling it.

Emotions: deeper, more present, than our language, than any words: lots of them, and unnameable. Stacked up in us before anything else, ready for a different world: reactions from forgotten earlier lives, existences. Species.

Poetry's a fudge, maybe it catches overtones, but its bright sound rings out and no one answers, no one's ever rescued, no ransom ever paid. No target's ever reached, no same spot touched, each word, each time – produces something different, unforetold. Or nothing. Zero.

Emotion. Sometimes it's the 'cheep cheep' of birds asleep.

I can't sleep.

I don't toss – I lie motionless. The emotions bubble on, a hot spring.

I have many emotions – they don't help, don't help me sleep nor stay awake. The animals have them. Like with us, emotion flickers over them permanently. Everybody has them, but they're probably the only thing that's yours, unconfessed and unpardoned. Hidden and irrelevant.

Anger: 'it makes me mad' ... I feel mad today ... Love: such love! – and now it's all gone by. What a fool ... what a bitch ... what a bastard....

Language sticks a cork in them, whatever they might be, alembics, the useless swirls and clouds, reactions like the octopus's blush.

The guy I overheard said: 'I must go early to the bank. My wife died in the night and if I don't go and close the account, the thieves will take it all. Like they took her.'

*

Doctor Chin – that beautiful body... Was Doctor Chin inside it? Thinking of other things, elsewhere: archaic skies, forgotten origins? Or swimming powerfully and breathing through some artificial gills?

*

'You can snore,' says Pietro, angrily. 'To snore is human. But you have symposia: 'Bonnie. Alcine.' 'If only....' 'I was wrong, I thought....' Enough, Hadar!'

*

Making a star would be a massive thing, bring us all extended life. But Doctor Chin – undersea: driving a chariot pulled by sharks – that's transformation. That's new life!

*

The village is small, silent. Something's going on. The villagers, survivors of some scourge, have faces of polished stone. No question of emotions here. I meet old fusion types

– the Tokamak crowd ... it won't work, and if it did, it would take years, and the energy field has utterly transformed.

It's the species – it's not resisting.... It flakes away, succumbs, mewls and splinters.

Publicity for fusion – that's my odd-job. A joke. It barely pays.

Pietro's doing well, I don't frequent him. After the catastrophe, the bandits moved in, and gave him work. They hold all the debt, decide who works, and works for them. He and his bank do very well.

We're all higgledy-piggledy, herded in from everywhere. I don't mention the ship – and no one's interested in our past.

Everyone needs company, even for a few minutes, and that's enough, absolutely.

Vanda's old, not ancient. She wears underwear preserved from youth – it gives her breasts and buttocks, stands her straight.

'You fancy an older woman, Hadar?' she says, up front. From afar you don't see her face is lines, and close to, very close, you don't see them either.

She smells of paper. 'I loved Shan State,' she says. 'When I worked there – the best, most loyal folk on earth.'

'It was drugs, Vanda,' I say, not committing.

'What else?' she says. 'Though we were clean. You use or you sell – what fool would use? You have fantasy, or you don't – no pill helps, and if you hurt – it's permanent.' She opens her arms, like Nike. 'Look at the art!'

Tattoos: all over. It's kitsch, cotton flowers, in bunches or in pictures. It's not primitive, just dull. I'm not an expert, but it's very dull.

She lies still as an adolescent – seen people like me labouring at her many times before. I think of Alcine, Bonnie, and it doesn't help.

'You must get used to old age, Hadar,' she says. 'If you don't, it will kill you.'

*

Pietro has a bright young friend, Clotilde. She's tough, guards your cash – no chance of loans. She and Pietro know who has the loot. There's lots. Mountains. No time to count it – it gets weighed.

A small silent village, giving orders to killers, fixers, over the hill. A city there, young guys with vans and lovelights, at dusk, making a parade. No blithe painted girl would go with them.

I often think of Doctor Chin. Thinking of absent people – it fills my time, it overfills. I need more time, and they recede, the shades, I need more time to think of them, to think of absent things in a non-existent way. It's all immaterial, of course – the flame, the air, the thought. I don't need search the times – nothing I think has ever happened....

Albert or Albertine – what difference might there be?

'Old age,' says Vanda. 'Don't think. You thought it all already. Don't use, don't think of pills or shooting up or fentanyl: time brings the pain, it grows – don't chivvy it. Make it your friend, your guardian, tutor.

'I'm satisfied, thinking, not thinking, of absent people. It's true, I don't think much of you – you're absent, but you've never been; never been here with me. It's going by – the colours, the white, the black: thought is without colour. Do you believe that, Hadar? What colour do you think? I suspect – you don't know, it's not occurred.

'It's reassuring, that you're trivial, Hadar. Reassuring for us both. Underwear! Your vision? Does that make you visionary?

'A star? There's so many, and you've been hitched to fantasy over just a tiny one.... You don't know how to fantasise: you print. It's realism that's your downfall. Copying. Reproducing – a sequence. Repetition. You're like the rest, Hadar, and your world is copies of itself, like you. You're a copy of yourself. You're a sliver of a species – a whole species looks out your eyes: a, a species being. A horrible failure. Everyman and someone else's underwear – it doesn't matter whose, or nobody's at all. What you exactly did not want. Trivial, like the rest. Species-being! What a con!'

'It's true,' I say. 'I'm limited. I objectify. I'm afraid, distorted, I miniaturise my peers, especially for sex. My vision's a dark tunnel. My star's a generator. That's what they are, all that they are.

'I'm an animal, that sniffs and pees. If I could describe what drives me, it's what's in sniff and pee. Describe that? – I'd be a genius. I can't.'

'Well,' says Vanda, 'don't cry. You never said that you were special. You got lucky – Doctor Chin gave you a whirl.'

'Which side were you on, Vanda,' I ask. 'The agency? The military?'

‘That’s for you to guess,’ she says. ‘And I’ll bet you’re wrong. I told you – the Shan, the loyalest people in the world. You think I’m opportunist?’

‘No, no, Vanda,’ I assure her.

‘Well, if you’re not, your insides wouldn’t work,’ she says. ‘Forget fusion. Forget the generator. It’s not your business to promote an inexistent thing. Let’s find out how this place works, and find a way to get us out of it.’

‘Wise words, dear Vanda,’ I tell her. ‘Stars. It’s always fascinated me, that little taradiddle by Browning – a star only you can see, and that must mean it’s yours. Like Tokamak has been for me – it’s not the fault of Browning, we’re all trite and trivial; it’s endearing. We did him at school, I think. But we’re stuck here ... like a ship on its stack of waves.’

I remember the ship: itself is destination, wherever it might go. And us, how do we get out, away, Vanda? We could roam and ramble, but for you and I, it would be all the same....’

‘Oh, we’d get the cash from Clotilde,’ Vanda says. ‘But – leave my flowers? All the years I’ve planted here? That isn’t trivial.’

‘You’re a pirate, Vanda,’ I say. ‘Like Crusoe. All the bible stuff, intoned to cover up – the slaving and the stealing.’

‘Maybe he had a star, they followed it, and they went on the rocks,’ says Vanda. ‘I learned – be very very careful when you’re with other people, even when they’re loyal.’

‘What do we understand, Vanda,’ I ask. ‘If we don’t know, face to face with one another....’

‘Trite, Hadar,’ she says. ‘Again. It shows you’re wrong. Here, the guys are tough and greedy. They’re not loyal. So when you speak of species – you're mistaken. It's a blind alley. 'Species' tells us we are a catastrophe. We are in conflict – women against women, women against men and vice versa, men dissolving men in acid. We need a galaxy of stars if each must follow one. You're imprisoned in your metaphor. Your fear of women, Hadar, determines you. Your fear – not of extinction of the species, but of yourself, your little province, before you've found you are incurable. Triteness ... not star-gazing, Hadar, not swimming in the deep....'

'If we leave,' I say, 'what do we hope to find?'

'Justice and equality,' she says, 'hanging by your thumbs. Me, wearing the *abaya.* Have a guess. What does sex teach you? Nothing – yet you run after it, in and out of season. You're earth, Hadar – the most you'll be is clay. Then dust.'

'Maybe Clotilde will give us cash and come with us,' I say. 'Pietro can't be fun.'

'He's a mint,' says Vanda. 'That's all the fun you need. But he sees the conflict that you don't. Rich and poor, ignorant and puzzled. Serfs and slaves. He laughs. It's almost wise – at least, it's canny. He's like Adil, the captain you told me – can steer but cannot stop nor start.'

'Your life is fable, Vanda,' I say, marvelling, 'where compromises have no weight.'

'Exactly,' she says. 'Keeping the story going. No stars. No holding breath. No breast strokes.'

I come to terms with my stupidity. It takes a minute. I'm transformed. No star. Justice and equality. No dress code, no religious cops, no repudiations, and no marriages – probably no kids. We'll start without a preconception of where we have arrived....

'Alas, Hadar,' says Vanda. 'You're enlightened, but you're ignorant. Even more than when you lived in fear and arrogance. This den of thieves, Hadar – they won't let us in, we're not the stuff they need: and so ... no regrets. If you can't be bad, be good. Be ascetic, if you can't stuff yourself with ravioli.

'I'll not seek justice, I'll just wear my clothes and flaunt my hair. You're forever starstruck. Put that aside. Tell the guy who runs the fusion ads to cool his act. Resign. Resigning from a job you haven't got – is easy....'

We think this over.

'Clotilde has a friend: Josiane. Maybe that's the bait,' says Vanda.

She's an inspiration. Why does she need me, I ask myself. What might I need to do? Banditry and milking goats? Either's outside my past....

'To me, Vanda,' I say, wanting to escape from her critique, my self-exposure, 'I have no remedy, but I know what is the question. The key – is it in the humans, their history, their mastery of the dialectic, that is, of themselves? Can we do what must be done, what we know we must? We, ourselves, for us....

'Or, as Engels said, are we in an infernal machine, a machination? An aimless process. A beginning but no end in sight, us, a storm-tossed jetsam; a cog of nature, tick-tocked in, telling no tale or time, born in dialectic of a nature mindless, careless, exploding into darkness...? That irrelevance, the universe, its whirligig is forever in us and beyond us. Nature – not just birds and raptors – dialectics too. Churning away, trying to make cheese out of water.'

'Well put,' says Vanda. 'You're a genius of digestion. The answer? I don't know. Which of your gurus? Who's right? I'd say both of you, but it can't be. You have to make up your mind – or somebody's. I can't.'

We leave it there, suspended over our consciousnesses.

*

'Don't think of leaving,' says Sandy, boss of the ad firm that handles fusion puffs.

'You don't pay me, Sandy,' I tell him. 'You must give. More money, brings forth more exaggerations.'

'Things are tight, Hadar,' he says. 'The past's as dark as unpaid bills: the future's wispy wills.... Pledge yourself to us. You're but a ticket in life's lottery – most numbers won't be drawn, will languish in the bag. The crucial thing is taking part. Otherwise, you'll never know – are you lucky? Or just lingering.'

'My old partner, Pietro,' I say. 'He thinks that. He thinks he's lucky. I am sceptical.'

'You have to be,' says Sandy. 'Until the draw. Then the excitement makes you pee your pants. That is the high spot in your life. You mustn't miss it, not for anything....'

'We've wandered off,' I say. 'From talking cash. That doesn't jog the numbers, but it buys the bag.'

*

Clotilde is neat. I say, ‘I’m one of Pietro’s oldest friends.’

‘He has no friends. He’s in his office,’ Clotilde says.

I see him looking out at me. He raises his hand – he recognises me. We have no business. He gestures – life is heavy with duties and rewards. There’s nothing more to say.

‘It may not interest you, Clotilde,’ I say. ‘I and my friend, Vanda – we want to leave. And maybe you do too....’

It’s weak. ‘Why don’t you take the bus?’ she asks.

‘We thought of something more definitive, more a rupture, a hiatus. A negation,’ I say. It’s not easy. I don’t know why Vanda wants her to come with us. Why don’t we take the bus.

‘We’re not safe here,’ she says. ‘And there’s Josiane. She works like me – over there. Here, if you don’t rob banks, you work in one. Both ways, it’s dangerous.’

‘Vanda is runic,’ I say. ‘But if she thinks it’s time to leave....’

‘It’s contacts, not runes, she registers’ says Clotilde, putting an amount of money in a large canvas bag. ‘I’ll get to be with Josiane. Vanda must think she can educate you, have fun too perhaps. I trust her – she was in Shan State, she says.’

At last – Pietro, and the ordinary world recede. It’s adventure. Am I precious to them? Or do they think I am the vulnerable one they must protect?

‘Pietro told me you were shipmates,’ Clotilde tells me. ‘He’s the captain here; in the bank, he broods. He must fear, inside. Old sailors, the ancients, go like that. They don’t feel they’re charmed – they feel they’re damned. There’s not much more to say.’

‘He didn’t say farewell,’ I say.

'Of course not,' says Clotilde. 'That's a mariner's curse. On ship, you don't make friends, not ever, it's a malediction, one of you will go. End really bad. There are so many ways at sea. Up the funnel, down the gangplank, wrapped in an ensign – or seagulls' breakfast. I know. All my friends, my family – they all went down on reefs. Or stuck in plastic shoals, forgotten and re-flagged, they hoped the albatros would show. They had the eye. Good shot! A royal dinner. Birds don't talk, Hadar – not like you. You talk too much. Those poets' wings – make them good targets. Like you, they don't bring tidings, glad or not. Those birds are toxic: they do for a whole crew....'

*

Maybe he loved me, Pietro: joshing me, to protect.

We'll never know.

Or just – he didn't care – sat in his counting-house, drinking Chivas Regal, the armoured glass reflects, like him ... staring at his end ... low-life, coming through the door, going out the bancomat.

*

'Now – nothing but cheerful looks, no talk,' says Vanda, handing out our steel-tipped staves. 'Remember, we'll see people scattered as we climb. They are real shepherds, but there's no real sheep.'

'They set a bearing on us,' says Clotilde. 'They've all been shipwrecked, down, then up, the foam, the white crests, foaming like sheepskins, soft carry them to shore: they say the waves are *moutonnant.* Sheeplike. A flock of wool.... Home again, homespun, shepherds' delight. They live in their nostalgia.... And their skin – it's slick: that bunker oil....'

We look down from the ridge. 'There's eagles sit up here,' says Vanda. 'But there's not much left to see. I expect they're bored – at home, stuck on shitty sticks, rolling their eggs.'

*

There's a horseshoe of grey and shining blocks. Some towers – limestone, perhaps. No sign of life.

'The university,' says Clotilde. 'You don't go there – people fired down from the towers. It's a place you tour, if you're a foreigner – you don't frequent. It isn't necessary....'

Vanda and I – we don't comment. It's not our world.

'Lifetime learning,' says Clotilde, 'means it's silly learning something before you get a job.'

'There's company on ships,' I say. 'Too much. The same. Too little. Except, you can paint, and at the end you start again.'

'The loneliness,' says Clotilde, 'that's the worst thing because it makes no sense. I joined a bank, but the customers are all frauds or gunmen. It's a battleship – I hoped it was a yacht.'

Vanda urges us on, she's bored. The silver river meets a horseshoe – a basalt wall. It trickles on, past, turbine-drunk.

'The dam was built, but there's no need,' Clotilde says. 'Electricity is plentiful ... besides....'

'I know,' I say. 'They never got to Tokamak.'

'There's nowhere here for us,' says Vanda. 'The people may be loyal, but they're all in their house. So what?' She prods us with her stick: 'On, on,' she shouts. 'Down the scree like moufflons, who falls first arrives the quickest –' and she skates and skids down the loose shale.

Clotilde – who seems revealed as a gloomy type, on about the sea on land, and probably the reverse – she whoops, she spreads her arms, her smock takes the wind and lifts her up – she sails, she bounces, her calico balloons – and the canvas bag spills open, round her head the notes and parchments flutter on their brilliant wings, lodge in the rocks, just disappear.

'Free!' she shouts. 'I'm innocent! My theft – has blown away....'

It makes no odds – in cities, carrying cash is the first step before you lose it, or are apprehended – as they say.

*

'Hurry, hurry,' Vanda says. 'This is no place for us. This town is worse than where we left. It's corporations, sheriffs with no cows and rustlers on the lurk. How they produce their wealth's a mystery, but when it's monetised, the thieves, the conmen, gather.... Alas, poor Josiane, Clotilde – the price they pay....'

*

'There is nothing that man fears more than a touch of the unknown.'

Elias Canetti

'What nonsense,' Vanda says. 'We're here to smother in it. The unknown....'

'The fear...?' I say.

'What nonsense,' Vanda says. 'Everything is unknown. But you're right – some of us live in fear of the inevitable. Nonsense, total nonsense. Look at Clotilde – she's ecstatic. She'll hunt our dinner for us – I'm just famished. She's the bird of wisdom just for now.'

It's true, Clotilde is transformed. She lopes along, she trips down a line of trees, they're low and billowy, and her cottony hair resembles theirs....

'Look!' she says, returning, carrying.... 'It's milk and cheese and cheese....' she says: that's all they make.

We're hungry, we don't ask if it's true the sheep aren't real – the cheese and milk are real enough.

'We could stay here,' Clotilde says. 'For ever. It suits me.'

Vanda and I concur. But all good things .... another day we spend, under the sun, climbing up grey basalt rocks, that cut our hands and knees. 'That stupid girl,' says Vanda. 'Not a shred of wisdom there....'

*

'This is the place,' says Vanda.

It doesn't thrill. Josiane has come – she's plump and puddingy, Clotilde sticks in her loving spoon – my! how they giggle – and it gladdens us. Sex is a quest for everything that's known, and those two hunt it down all night like raptors. Sex – a journey into nowhere, except it – alas – defines the species. All more or less identical....

The house is one of many abandoned here. Vanda and I share a damp bed – a bolster for us both, light as a *Windbeutel* – and all night I think of Doctor Chin – five fathoms just a paddle, the dark eyes blank behind the goggles.

Play 'loves me, loves me not' on starfish arms ... What do they know?

How Vanda snores, the dampness of the mattress seeps into my heart.

Oh no – I realise, she wants to make a Shan Sate here. The people here are loyal. The art? Those green and scarlet fruits of marzipan ... they're cute, but dull. They're very dull.

*

'Getting here was a laugh,' says Vanda. 'Now we must organise.'

'Not Shan State, Vanda,' I implore.

'The army? And the trade?' she says. 'No, absolutely not. Asking for trouble, giving it and receiving it. Why, Hadar, is that what you want?'

'I don't believe you're offering it,' I say. 'Enough for me to know there are loyal people there.'

'I've tried to tell you,' Vanda says. 'Your Tokamak's a waste of time – your tiny captive star will not be born. As for the deep – my lung is weak. Besides – a glaucous world, eternal darks ... the silence, just those cheeps and burps, the electronic minimals, nickels and dimes of sound, the fallen angel fish – no, absolutely not for me. Sit as a sponge? Waving a thousands arms, digesting by hugs – or living in somebody's old shell.... No, no, we're better here.

'The idea is to find a way, a vision, if you like, that isn't star and isn't wet, not sea nor sky....'

'And what is that, Vanda?' I ask. 'Josiane and Clotilde are credit – they take life in. When you give them cash, it disappears.... What's your vision? Debt? Parcelling it out to favourite schemes? You'd join the robbing hoods dressed as a philanthropist. Is that what you want? Benevolence?'

'You're harsh, Hadar,' she says, and laughs.

The village has one street, a valley, with alleyways that sidle up the hills. It's not Shan State.

Too soon to be the end, but we're faltering....

'The people, Vanda, what did they do here?'

'Work in the peanut factory,' she says. 'Like now.'

If you don't buy debt, nor sell it – what's left is to forgive it. For that you need a lot of cash.

'Our money blew away,' I tell her.

'Then we'll need to work,' she says cheerfully. 'The peanut factory....'

'It seems you planned it so,' I say, appalled.

'I am a saviour,' Vanda says. 'I'm in the saving line. I ride the contradictoriness.... I saved you, Hadar. Clotilde and Josiane can know a passion Pietro would exclude, rejecting Clotilde, who's pretty. Josiane is smart – not smart enough to leave aside Clotilde, but then – one's redeeming power is limited, just like my sacrifice....'

It's a revelation. Vanda proposes, and disposes. Her plan is not a vision – it's for us! We three or more, we – the rudderless, the drifting everyday....

'The peanut factory, Vanda,' I say at last. 'It's a trap!'

'Accustom yourself, Hadar. It's all a trap, from Tokamak to saluting kingfish, therein lies your genius, your talent, will to live – however you have read about life's aims, and chosen one that sounds more appetising, off the rack for you....'

It's terrible! A confession that repudiates.... 'Oh fuck! Vanda,' I shout. 'You're normal, as they say. You're dull. You're very dull! In Shan State – you must have played both sides....'

'Oh no,' she says, hardly reacting. 'I'm very loyal. Loyalty before everything. I was loyal to oaths, and to other people's loyalty.'

'That's what I mean,' I say. 'To the Shan, and to the Agency.'

'Everybody does like me,' she says. 'The Agency, the Shan, they did. To make your way, you need an army and a state – get used to that, Hadar. I had nothing like that, nothing at all. I'm ordinary – that means I'm right. I know process: you *are* poetry. Quite unlike me. The dialectic – a unicorn....'

'What process, Vanda?' I ask, thinking of the mystery, Tokamak. How the universe was populated with generators....

'Peanuts,' she says. 'And it's not simple. What to do with the shells.... Can't throw them under the seat like you did, Hadar. Move on! forget the revelation you had with Doctor Chin.'

*

When you leave, you must have somewhere you can go....

'What are you, Hadar?' Vanda shouts, pushing me out the rented house – already we owe rent:

'You're not a scholar. Too scared to be a libertine. A pander? An aspiring pimp, eyeing up women, men – hoping to make a buck by selling on to someone powerful?'

'That's harsh, Vanda, that's very harsh,' I say. I don't resist. It might be so – and then?

I rush out of the poor house, push past the liberated couple, the cashiers: Clotilde, a creature fashioned for the world of man ... and Josiane, conceived by nature – froglike. Then I reflect again on my inadequacies, eternal second-rate. What was I to Doctor Chin...?

And Pietro: his vulgar fecklessness, the dirty dog ... my brother, lookalike....

'Off already, Hadar?' asks Josiane. 'We thought to give Vanda another day. Then leave.'

Everybody quits. My loyalty: who can tell what you are loyal to? Maybe I'm loyal to Clotilde – it's not an obsession. Vanda did me a favour – that's the end of it – it's not an oath.... Clotilde asks, 'Did we keep you awake last night, rough and tumble?'

'No, no,' I say. 'I keep myself awake.'

*

What's here for me? Peanuts?

*

'Leaving?' asks a guy: Selim. 'Don't fancy the peanut factory? It's intricate – the roast, the salt, and then disposing of the shells – a masterwork. It's for TV. Some people can't watch without them.... Has there been a crime, that you go so soon?'

'Only theft,' I say. 'Condoned. Complicity – can't be a crime. It's knowledge and friendship. Betrayal – that's serious, but there's no law.'

'It can be good here,' Selim says. 'Not every day. You have to understand the process – the new modalities of thought and application. If you think Sufi-like – maybe you do, my friend – life will be sad, you will be contrary, contested too.'

'No,' I say. 'I'm fragments. Bits of *maschilismo*, I'm afraid. I'm shamed. Progressive, regressive – in equal parts.'

Selim moves away.

I think of Doctor Chin.

*

Selim shouts: 'Be very careful if you climb the rocks. The cops may shoot – and then the shepherds, spies! they'll fish you in.... Crooks....' We laugh.

'The factory,' I say. 'It's science: today's, and everyone in white. With sneakers too.'

'Ah yes,' he says. 'But – if it all explodes – the facility, and peanut butter over everything?'

I think – suppose my captive star explodes – leaks out, agglomerates: a thousand suns of heat close above our heads.... 'There's nothing in the books that covers that, nothing the sages, or the doctors of the law....' he wavers, peters out.

I'm nonplussed too....

'I can't endure,' he says. 'The waiting till they take us to the sea, start having us adapt to life down there. The latest deal. There isn't work, not as we know: you swim around, there's food just lying, swimming too, little mouthfuls, canapés, abounding everywhere. You float along in schools, but mostly what you do – it isn't learned. You pick it up.... There's wonders of instructors, teach you how to have a streamlined look....'

I think of Doctor Chin. My pilot fish.

'Suppose we go together, Selim – up the rocks, and then you'll see the sea,' I say. I need protection, company. 'You could sit upon the shore, a barnacle upon its rock, and wait....'

'An adventure?' Selim says. 'With a good end. Who could object?'

'You trust, Salim,' I say, 'perhaps too much. You think, the latest science – it must be the best, and all the rest is just approximation, destined soon to become poetry. But the best, the latest – that in turn will be improved, discarded, museumised....'

'It's life,' says Selim. 'You must trust in life, Hadar!'

He knows already that I don't.

*

Selim labours up the rise. 'Up, up, up!' I shout. 'The rocks are structured like a language, you must talk to them, use your tongue, Selim – and howl! Inflate: your lungs will balloon and bear you up! Shout! A slogan ... oath, declaration of your faith, that you can float and rise....'

'Not a sentence – a verse!' he says, leaping upwards, inspired. 'Poetry is faith, and faith has prepared us all to welcome every new experience, invention, obstacle – in peace....'

I start to say 'wise words –' but only 'wise' comes out – a type in buskins and leather breeches, a curving stick held as a threat above his head – blocks our way. We should have kept quiet and toiled....

'Why? This is a frontier,' he says. 'You need a motive and a document to cross....'

'Nonsense,' says Selim. 'It's all one place, everywhere is... A "here" is here for everyone, and "there" as well....' and as he blathers this, the guy brings down his stick, and whacks Selim's bare head.

The rocks are poised untidily, like a text in solid geometry, with five sides, seven, nine – I hadn't meant to pull him down before he struck me too – but down he goes, and bounces, slides and cuts – I think of Clotilde, her goat-girl skills ... she'll never fall, she'd float....

He lies, a heap of homespuns, leathers, fleece....

We run, we hop. Don't look back – bad luck....

This is the crime we run up from – the blot on our tales, we two.

We're complicit, the crime – a lifetime of uncertainty – the guilt, my guilt – now glows, now gutters, now flares up, and dies....

'Quick!' I say. 'Wounded or dead, he's quicker than us two.... For sure, he's following, he's after us, he won't give up, not ever.'

*

We scutter down the other side. The village is the old one that I left. It's like the other one I left as well, but new to Selim. He'll see it as familiar – except the main street's full of banks – there's twenty-six – a nest of branches like a monkey-puzzle, and at the end a cemetery. Maybe he's right – nothing is new or old.

'The sea, the sea!' I say. 'Sit by the sea, Selim!' And so he does.

*

We know ourselves through some unintended act, that marks us like a brand. What was the intention of the unintended, what are we, to have acted in that way? Why? Why do it, anything, why did it happen? Common sense? Instinctive self-defence? Violence? – a predisposition ... or generosity of love or hate or fear? A hidden spring: Unthinking? How to live with consequences that have no cause....

Selim is terrified, he's right. I'd be so myself, except his reaction is so fierce, so total, it takes my attention, holds it –

to see him, bending, shaking, 'All he wanted, Hadar, was some cash,' he says.

'He could have fallen, Selim,' I say. 'No one can say now: – it's out of our hands, it's history.'

'You haven't understood,' he says. 'We're watched. We're the immortals – everything we do is on the record – if they care. It all depends. Don't rant: being recorded, followed – it's not because of science – you did what you did because of you. Those cameras are conscience....'

I must distract him. My second crime – deception.

'I regret leaving Vanda,' I say. 'She reminds me of Simone Signoret. Now, there was a star – it its time, of course. That old movie....'

'Nothing is old,' Selim interrupts. 'There's context, that's all. Peace, Hadar. You forgot. The good shepherd – maybe he was bad, or paid. It isn't up to you.' He hunches on his rock.

*

'I'll fix it,' Pietro says. He doesn't leave his office, shouts through the closed glass door. 'You, the innocent,' he says and laughs. 'In trouble!'

There's a notice on the bank door. 'Wanted: Clotilde'. I hear Pietro's taken over all the other banks.

*

'What disaster,' says Selim: he's trembling, but he doesn't cry now. 'What have you done, discovered, Hadar? Now a death, our guilt, our flight, eternal....'

‘Oh,’ I say. ‘I have an answer. Nothing is your fault. And nothing mine. The answer – if you wait, may come out of the sea.’

Will Doctor Chin be recognisable? And recognise me still? ‘Or out the sun. A replica that we can tame, put in a shell and play with like a golden ball....’

*

‘Fishcakes,’ says Pietro. They are. Oatmeal cast as pilchards, burnt deep brown. ‘We should have a party, you, me, and Selim. Whistle up Clotilde – her arms – a money net. She had the eye. She watched the seagulls, the currents – others trawled or shot their nets – but her arms – charmed the money in. A party – she loves those – it’s all a source of wealth.... Not even, not ever, hers. Just business, quantity. Now – I guess you two are straight, not even making-do.’ We don’t respond to his vulgarity. He goes on, ‘You must have your reasons – so, we’ll drink and paint stick figures on the walls, having an orgy ... giraffes can come in at the visual end....’ He laughs. We, Selim and I, we don’t.

It’s evident, that sado-mas attracts the banking class.

‘You’ve understood,’ says Pietro. ‘It’s best not to go out, fish stuff out the sea. Let it alone. You could dredge up the future, before it’s time has come.’

I think of Doctor Chin.

‘How do we live, meantime?’ asks Selim.

‘If the bandits sweep down from the hills,’ Pietro says. ‘They’ll maybe find the cash that Clotilde so carefully bound up. I dug a vault beneath me, though, to hide the choicest treasures. If it's intact – it'll last us all our lives.'

'It's not what I had hoped,' says Selim. 'But it's not all bad.'

It doesn't work like that. Nor did fusion.

*

Pietro takes a dipper, fills it from the sea. 'Here,' he says. 'It's aquavit. I've nothing stronger –' But it's strong.

'You know back stories, Pietro, like on the ship. What it was for, and why we were not into it....' I say.

'Oh, I bodge,' he says, and laughs. 'The bank is where all secrets rest. Hope and fears, crimes and redemption. You, Hadar – your adventure with Vanda, the climbing up and down the rocks ... you re-enact the "Interpretation of Dreams". Anxiety – this is the age. Nothing is natural, nothing grows quite carelessly, resigned or optimistic – dither, Hadar. Uncertainty, the wanting what can't be, and wishing not to be exactly what you are. You've no defences.... Selim – is gullible. Gullible when he had the faith, now when he wants his apostasy to give him revelation, he expects an utter change.'

'It's true,' I say, 'the rocks, the climbing and the crime. Vanda, Clotilde and Josiane – all courted, all rejected in a day....'

'Whoa, there, old horse,' shouts Pietro, laughing wildly. 'Forget analysis! Wait! See what the future brings, and if the future works. Your bio is just trivial, Hadar....'

We drink the sea. It makes us sick. The midday sun hammers us. We lie like sea-lions, legless and roaring on the sand – if bandits come, they'd break the bank.

*

'Joy,' says Pietro. 'Money, my business – it reminds you of shit, it's infantile, but it's pleasure, pleasure in yourself, your defence, your play.'

'I can't agree,' says Selim. 'I believe, if you want life, you must prepare for war. And then desert.'

'Oh, people get tired of fighting wars,' Pietro says. 'Here, they've had wars against everything – against themselves, the animals, the weather, against blame and against commitment.... What has it accomplished? *Enrichissez-vous*! Play with your cash! It's real and true, it's not experiment, and not hypothesis. See, I can print it out....'

And so he does – we've left the shore, sit in his office, drinking schnapps. Tequila, with much salt. We drum our feet to hear the echo down below, the hidden vault reverberates; the reserves! There they are, the reinforcements, – the press to print more notes, the moneyers to test the coin ... assayers to try the fineness of the gold....

'We deal in futures here,' says Pietro, swivelling in his chair, 'but it's a fraud. We've no idea if there will be a future. It's the best way, Hadar: trust in time's boomerang ... once tossed, it must return. See what climbing rocks has done for you. Adventure? Leaving Vanda, your safe house. You're lost and guilty.'

'You're a primitive, Pietro,' I say, irritated. 'You have aggression in you, not enjoyment. Your civilisation – is poison. *Homo homini lupus* Man is a wolf to man. I shan't defend you.'

'You're full of contradictions,' Pietro says. 'No matter. Do what you want, what protects you from your self-destructiveness.'

He bangs out a list of numbers on his cranky Burroughs. 'The fish poison con,' he says. 'That'll be what we have got. This nausea.... Just lie back, Hadar, enjoy the silver bullets, you're innocent, they've no effect ... and oops! Bad shot, you crap your pants ... there's a run, a glut, of silver fish sporting in my rolls of credit paper....'

'This brine,' says Selim, half laughing, half puking, 'Too strong for me.'

We're pissed.

We don't commit to saving Pietro. Or maybe we did long ago, and then forgot.

*

'Save me,' Pietro says. 'Defend me. They all know exactly who and where we are.'

'I told him that,' says Selim, pulling away from me. 'Hadar is frivolous, light as pastry.'

I think, 'I must get rid of Selim. He's a dreamer. Anyone can dream, and at the same time be ignorant.'

'Look,' says Pietro. 'These crises and catastrophes. Everyone's demoralised – long stretches filled with nothing – life spools out, you die. If you're lucky, there's a bag for you.

If not – naked in the pit. The wise man sees there's money, and above all power, made free and easy at these times. The old die off, the sociable croak first, the rich donate and hope that charity will save their health. I'm a plodder, as you know – but I have what it takes....'

'Is that a billow?' Selim asks, trying to stand, and waving at the sea. 'A shell. A naked virgin with long hair – or a tornado, spinning into rage....'

'Relax, Selim,' says Pietro. 'It'll be an artificial whale. I've arrived at power and money, that's the nub – no virgins wanted there.'

'That's dull, even for you, Pietro,' I say, annoyed. 'There's observing, and inventing. Not to mention love: design, and economic modelling....'

'I've not found anything at all but power and cash,' he says. 'Or – cashpower, to simplify. The rest you do in your spare time. The other routes – there's Freud, "Jew without God". Examining ourselves, and our malaise. He ended bad, traduced. There's fusion, Hadar; following your star. Or diving, Selim: mind the hooks, and tell Hadar to mind the crooks!'

He laughs, knowing all there can be known about a tiny world.

'Someone should send me back Clotilde,' Pietro says. 'She'll make up the company. Not Vanda, though.... I don't need her. No ordinariness. Selim – you're still innocent, you could leave.... Take ship: round the point – you're there. No climbing, don't go far from shore ... things disappear, it's called the deep, that's how. It's treacherous, there's monsters

... the sea itself is monster number one, the mother of them all that splash and slither.'

'It sounds to me, Pietro,' I tell him. 'This is ordinary greed, space to enjoy it in, and power to keep you safe.... Vanda found inspiration in Shan State – is this why you don't want her here? She knows too much.... Is yours a tiny state, Shan State?'

There is a pause, with Pietro wrinkling his face. Then, he says, 'This is not my name. Nor yours are yours. This is not the place, the country, that we washed up in.... All's different, all's anonymous. Other people will motivate and threaten us.... We symbolise for them – lost riches, lost enjoyment, attenuation of the word and disappearance of the faith – all faith, in stars and rocks and reefs....'

'I love that,' says Selim. 'I was lost, now I'm in the fold....'

'... we're all they fear, and all they've lost,' Pietro says.

Selim: we truss him up, put him in the boat, start it up, and fix the wheel.

'That way, you can't be caught by tentacles or mermaids, no Circe can undo out knots,' I say, thinking of how, if he's left free, one black and starry night, black as a newt, all rubbery, my Doctor Chin might climb aboard, recruit him, draw him down, and down he'd be transmogrified – a super-swimmer, cutting the water like a gutting knife.... Chancing on hopeful eggs, and casual – he'd fertilise them, he'd be a patriarch of crabs ... Santa Claws....

We're very drunk. Some party! No women and no fights – I try to share my insights and my jokes....

'You have to take the oath,' Pietro says. 'I am your motherland. Love me and die for me. Freud saw it all, and would have lived it too.... Screw her like she would screw you....'

'The universe,' I say, 'is an abundance. Each of us can have their star.'

'Bring me Clotilde,' Pietro shouts. 'I'll make a tiny state, a Vatican, my switzers – recruited from Shan State....'

The drunken king? Or the pure hunter, Tshibinda, 'I prefer to hunt an animal, rather than to hunt a man,' I say.

'No,' says Pietro, laughing loud. '*Kutumboka!* I'll wave the bloody heads of enemies, and dance the dance of victory! Not Tokamak, you idiot, Hadar – *kutumboka!*'

Selim is passive – and we push him off. They send up rockets, round the point. 'Dear Clotilde,' Pietro says. 'Her bagging coin and wadding notes – there is no peer.'

*

It's all too small for me.

*

Every nighte and alle
The fire will burn thee to the bare bane
Luke-Wake Dirge

'Selim's an indestructable,' says Clotilde, the new queen. 'They fired on him, his boat – thinking it was an invasion, or a plague ship. He sang. "I dwell in the bosom of the deep...."

Quite inappropriate. As for Pietro – he wants to break us up, me and Josiane – I'll persecute him, and,' she turns to me, 'for the time being – *Josiane is yours!* Safe-keeping, or it's me you'll reckon with.'

'Greek fire!' says Selim. 'You drunks didn't tell me – only about the mermaids. I saw lots of those – in black, with gas-masks, snorkels, trying to climb aboard....'

'And did one have a doctorate?' I ask, jealousy thick as polenta in my veins. 'Sleek and sapient?'

'Fire everywhere,' says Selim, not responding. 'Fire on board. The ocean was ablaze – the water, slick and black – all's sleek – the fish, the birds, the newt-like creatures....'

'And was it all consumed?' I ask, in dread and expectation. 'The water? Did you see the rocks, the wrecks, the pearls, the bones, all blackened, all exposed...?'

I fear for Doctor Chin. But – the earth! Without the seas – just land, so we can spread, and plant and toil ... sizzle and sweat and procreate, the palmtrees in the deepest rifts and trenches....

The sun! Our star – a conquest, fusion triumphant, and the seas – quite dried and putrid, the sand fusing into clessidras, tear-bottles, toddy-glasses.... Our star, triumphant – the rotting deep, the new and putrid land ... our hope, our pestilence.... Those dessicated mariners....

'Oh no,' says Selim. 'Shells there were, abounding, from their artillery....'

All those creatures ... instead of being hauled up one by one, explored and taunted by the bathyspheres – everybody's Doctor Chin, Professor Hoover, hung out to dry and smoked and opened wide .... all massacred at once. A great injustice –

there's one every minute, like a metro train, but this, miraculous *mazzata* of the lot, more than a continent – and intercontinent – massacre of species, like tuna in a barrel, the *tonnara,* a *mattanza*, a fable of our own, our, end....

'Oh no,' says Selim. 'The sea was in its place – just lightly singed, maybe some roast sardines, some water boiled, dead sea – some soles in flames....'

*

> 'The *real barrier* of capitalist production is *capital itself.'*
>
> Karl Marx

'You see, Clotilde,' I say – we're sitting very close together on the divan, though to proximity I usually give no heed – 'We've lost some chance to skip ahead. It's Pietro – he's frivolous, and unpredictable. He thinks he knows how to keep the robber barons, his clients – the peasant anarchists, the bandits – the patriarchs, of whom he is the senior patriarch ... in check. The accumulation is in his primitive – his archaic – hands. Progress, Clotilde. If you don't believe in that, then human history is a scattering, a random slouch. Pietro – whom I respect and serve – is the obstacle, unconscious, to a more secure future for us all.'

Clotilde – true unthinking servant, even slave, of capital – indifferent to its theories and philosophy – I feel her breath on me. My hand touches hers. I remember Selim say 'I'm in the fold' – the text I'm lecturing from, somehow it folds.

'Bonnie,' I say, 'you remind me so of her, but she was cold, and you are warm, Clotilde. You're dangerous, of course – you're Pietro's girl – he's terrible and wild, but he withdraws.... He's absent – maybe in his nodule, on the way to stars. He's in his office always, doing sums, printing them on that machine....'

Our hands are joined. It cannot be. Though – I respect her too, her choice ... if it's a choice of me; you can't insult, spring back alarmed.

'Yes?' she asks. 'And what did you and Bonnie do?'

'Not much,' I say. Clotilde doesn't seem to care.

'And Josiane?' I ask.

'Yes,' says Clotilde, and that is it.

*

It is a dreadful thing, but in the situation, quite unstoppable.

'Oh no!' says Selim, with a little laugh and covering of mouth.... 'Don't mention ever ... you and Pietro's woman.... It's crouching on an open razor – no! on a buzz saw....'

'There are seeds of revolution in those "Forms",' I say. 'The tyranny of Pietro....' I gabble on, as if I'm echoing some lesson from long past. 'Gives way. "The whole of the bourgeoisie will now rule on behalf of the people...."'

'That's us,' Clotilde says. 'We're the people and the bourgeoisie.'

'It's true,' I say. 'But we must be very careful. Is that exactly what we want? Another empire? More service in the deserts....'

'No,' says Clotilde. 'Right now, I want a something else that's absolutely different.'

And so we do.

It's regrettable. It's not: it's perilous. Equivocal, delicious. I tell her of the murder, up in the rocks, and Doctor Chin.... She seems quite fascinated, though it doesn't show at all.

'It's quite incredible,' she says. 'You're clumsy – but you're not conspiratorial. You're untried, fresh as fresh lychee.'

We certainly don't plot – Pietro is in place, takes all responsibility: we are his vassals for the while – 'We're the party of Order,' I tell Clotilde, and she's amused.

'"Should this torture then torment us Since it brings us greater pleasure?"' she asks, greatly delighted. 'I love a little underhand,' she says.

I'd always thought Pietro superficial, even on the ship, in the inflatable, now even more – as lord or emir – guardian of a tiny enclave, a treasure house so rich great powers combine to keep him upright and defended.

'As things are, Clotilde,' I say, 'there's no development, no progress. We're Pietro's guard dogs. He grows rich, richer – aspiring to be richest....'

'Development? You don't want any. You're a backwater,' she says, quite affectionate.

I hear 'black water'. 'No,' I say, 'I have the star. That would be progress, liberation. Heat without moisture. No dynamoes – just glow.

'So, Doctor Chin, the modifying us, our species, fiddling variations on our evolution – I've come to see it as a fantasy, regression. A deviance.'

'You dramatise, you talk things up,' she says. 'There's no point in new analysis, it was all done over a century ago. There's big and little pools scattered all over, ruled by miniscule King Storks – reactionary chancers who bang their opposition up .... Best if they're wealthy, or administer a mound of gold – there's money for us lick-spittles....

'Banks, oil, minerals and taxes ... corporations and foundations, ruins and towers – little states and tiny towns, countries flaked from countries, enclaves, exemptions, autonomies, holy cities and profane – escapes and hidey-holes ... set up as exemptions that can make a buck, or keep one safe....

'It's good. For me and you, it's the best thing that will ever happen, but there'll be hard times, there always are, and then there'll be some even harder ones....'

'You do your work so well....' I say.

'What else?' she says: 'You'd need be stupid not to be able to....'

*

There's microstates, artillerymen in drag: royalties and holy rollers – doing flits, speaking in tongues – guys in black togas fleeing from the cops.... Throwing up ramparts – fiefs untouchable, with rules arcane. The world is one: and immediately, the body impolitic liquifies... each cell has its own constitution and liberties. We are one such. A bandit state: without our loyalty; with cash and infinite pretensions.

It's very good. I'm captain of the guard, ordering myself stood down. Clotilde shuts her guichet – we hug, we cling, and play naked and enthralled, at being one and indivisible....

*

'This boat,' says Pietro, lurching out his office – 'Is very hard to steer. Too bad that Captain Adil, who knew that manoeuvre well, can't join with me – for I can stop and start, but can't steer a course. Or tack.'

*

'You're excitable, Hadar,' says Clotilde. 'But not exciting. I was first lady, now I'm first and second. What might that mean? In and out? Faithful and rebel?'

'It sounds fine to me,' I say.

*

Selim's still shaking. 'Star shells: they were over me and underneath. 'Bombs bursting in air'.

'They've got the same idea as us, up the gulf – a little state, with everybody loyal. A speciality: casino ... whores ... even the sunset – with clear skies, the stars....'

It's a tragedy, of course: the species is ingenious, rushing down the slope, to fragmentation, dissolution, re-thinking. I rethink.

*

'Clotilde,' I say. 'When passion's spent, what can we offer? Move us away from cash and Pietro.

'Winds of change and tempests of revolt – the guys who haul the cash and don't get paid: they're feisty....'

'Yes,' she says. 'We have that gleam, the two of us, a revelation. Not a single star – a firmament. Not an adaptation – an eternity....'

'Conversion!' – we both say the word together. Faith and rigour. A pole star – hope that springs, and once a week's renewed.

'It sounds a little tawdry,' says Clotilde. 'But it is the longest practice humans have devised, to keep us in our ranks, singing and chanting – the same rhymes and harmonies. Faith. Up and down this coast – the rules, and then the "getting round the rules" – like everywhere. We shall be Goldilocks, who is the virgin bird of wisdom – entering, sleeping with all the bears, eating their food, letting them growl and fight it out – "What's the true faith", they ask, "That isn't superstition or a blasphemy"... and "How can I duck the faith, do what I want?".... Think Goldilocks, dear Hadar – her story's aprocryphal, but widely read....'

'Short and simple, Clotilde. I suggest the word of Obadiah....' I say, inspired.

'Beatles? That's all uplift – we need the fear of – something imminent. Selim's pilgrimage, to carry me back here. Shooting stars, boiling seas, not Obladee ....'

'Not that,' I say. '"As thou hast done, it shall be done unto thee." That's it, all you will need. No introspection, no theology. A promise and a threat. It's all there – like in Freud. Life, and in its bud – death. The threat's the promise.'

'You mean religion?' Selim asks. 'That's on the skids. Even a new one – it's just frighteners and hoods. And whips.'

'Sacrifice,' Clotilde says. 'We're always urged to that, to change our life and live austere. Well, mine's already much like that. And "Wait!" Wait for the price to fall, wait till we find the cure, wait – we'll see if seas cool down, or animals return.... "We'll find the answer with more cash – donate and trust...."'

'That's jesuitry,' I say. 'What you describe. It's superficial. I know about the "promise, promise", from our Tokamak. It's all too generalised – peole say "yes", think "no", "not in my lifetime". You cannot be obedient to someone else's aspirations, or their guess....'

'Then get Pietro to pay out more,' she says. 'Real sums, not crusts and stamps.'

'That works as well,' says Selim. 'Your quiver. Fill it with many darts, and poison some....'

'The trouble is Hadar,' Clotilde says, turning on me. 'He's scuffed these leaves so many times.... Invention of the new: really, it's just a polish and a lacquering of ancient brasses.... We need something fresh and new and innocent. Hadar is worn coin: a Maria Teresa dollar, copied, re-minted time and again.... 'No more a Ulysses – no more ancient reluctant mariners, cynical and homebody. Find someone new and willing. Josiane! Let's bring her here – assume I'm Queen Boran – anomalous, but with all the tricks and treats.... But – who will make the trip?'

'It's true,' says Selim. 'I quake. I'm an acolyte who needs a reassurance, a cosmology that says "all will be well". I'm not taking ship again. If Hadar isn't current coin – let him go!

He's already shown aggression – he's the warrior.... Off with him!'

*

> *'Eh bien, c'est tout, qui me répugne et qui me dégoûte à présent! Pas seulement toi! .... Tout! L'amour surtout! ...'*
>
> Louis-Ferdinand Céline, *Voyage au bout de la nuit.*

'Right!' I say. 'I'm Robinson outcast. I have to make the journey, past the scene of my unspeakable, my continuing, crime: its aftermath, my guilt.'

'And hurry,' Clotilde says. 'We need – something to die for! A cause. An end. A home – a birthing ... a compass in the brain – for migration, a salmon's summons from the wild, the scripted destiny.... Bring me Josiane....'

Disgruntled, with an infinite bad grace, I arm myself, start toiling up the rocks....

*

There's no one, no shepherds, no chamois, moufflons, skittering silent down the rocks. If they speak – they could lose their concentration, a moo a baa – and down they'd go. But, anyway – they are not here.

There's Josiane – asleep, the Book of the Dead lies open on her chest. I'm tired – I lie beside her. That unpaid rented room, the damp crawling over everything, a blob, an omelette of a web, a mushroom-insect. I sleep. This, where I lie, is Clotilde's place. Maybe Vanda's – who must be at work, busy and bent, not earning rent – spending it all on aquavit....

Josiane – she smells of booze. There's bottles, pills.... On the table, there's the 'Elementary forms....' What is she? New Age? Old Age? A swot for some exam in banking – 'cultural preparedness'...?

Maybe I die.

I resurrect.

Robinson, the obtuse bastard, slaver, proto- and post-fascist too.... That's me!

'Forget all that, Josiane,' I say, distressed.

She wakes! That book is heavy on her....

'It's just for fun,' she says. 'Reading the books. That is the easy part of life. Write one yourself, read two. The two you read, two of a pair, beat the rubbish in your inky hand....'

'We need you, Josiane,' I say.

'Clotilde needs me,' says Josiane. 'I knew she would.'

'You're the philosopher,' I say. 'You take it in your stride. We need a pole-star, a shining magnet pulling our gaze, a twinkling to dance to, round the summer fire....'

'Love,' she says, sleepily, pulling me towards her, over her. A quilt.

'No!' I say, withdrawing quick. 'We've had enough of that.'

'It's not what you are thinking of,' she says. 'Not love coupled with a subject. Desire! Unrequited, infinite and permanent. The nothing, the gravity that makes you spin and burn.'

'Expand the thought, Josiane,' I say. 'Write Vanda a goodbye – and up the rocks....'

Vanda – of course, is in the factory. Lined up, where it all began, beside the four star US generals, hostages and renegades, rolling spliffs and packing them in boxes like contraband cigars. Shan State coronas.... Packing those little bouncy mines that kiddies love collecting – inside, instead of tiny dynamited darts – fresh tabs. Warm still, from the chemist's saucepan....

'Stop dreaming, Hadar,' Josiane says. 'Now, carry me. That way they'll never stop us – they'll see you are a good shepherd, bringing mercy to a stranded sheep.'

The strand.... I think of Doctor Chin, the strokes, powerful as waves.... Like Tokamak, the idea was right – and then? And then? A murky goggled life....

*

'Listen, Josiane,' I say. 'I've given up almost the lot – love went first, then vision, hope ... Now, why must I carry you?'

'If you were a ship, you'd carry both of us,' she says. 'A bus. An aeroplane – the carrying would be gratuitous – ferried over water, earth and air. Now – carry me! Show you're the good shepherd.'

Clambering on these basalt blades – my sheep aloft – her hooves are sharp, she digs them in, her nails ... nail me – she lies across my shoulders.... A lost sheep, definitively found.

She wears a fun fur – we're both very hot. 'The poem dealt with desire,' I say. '"O fleece! locks cascading to my collar”.... But, desire and evocation of the common sort: paid sex in perpetuity.’

‘No temples, statues, nothing built,’ she says. ‘Processions. A striving for death and life. No one to give or take away. Unbridled want, insatiable....’

‘And Pietro?’ I say. ‘People want the boss to give them things....’

‘Oh,’ says Josiane. ‘The boss is quite irrelevant. This one or that – it’s quite indifferent. No one can know your want. It’s abstract, seeking after abstract things. Freedom? You’re always free to want – your life is like an empty jug. You need it so’s to fill with what you want, that’s always bigger than the jug – hotter, colder, rarer, wriggling – it has no shape, no name. Even if you think you have it, it can fit the jug.... You try – just stuff it in ... it’s not at all the satisfaction that you sought.... You want more life, and what comes closer in your search – is death. For all and everything. You’ll get the opposite of what you want....’

‘And that’s what keeps us all together, Josiane?’ I ask. ‘What we refined types call society?’

‘You’ve been on a ship,’ she says. ‘All that you want, everyone on board – is not to sink, to dock somewhere ... to go on shore and rent a whore, to drink and break up bars – and then it’s ship-time once again. You’re at the start once more – both, the stoker and the helmsman. Wanting, Hadar. Religion, politics, sex, and treasure hunts ... the same, the same, the same want.... Never fulfilled....’

She keens. She’s tough and heavy. Demanding, too. We reach the crest.

‘Look down,’ she says. ‘On either side. The world’s all villages. Much the same.’

*

‘What’s this,’ asks Pietro, as I set her down. ‘A sacrifice? For me?’ He’s quite displeased. ‘A sheep? – see what a fat tail!’

‘The idea is hers,’ I say. ‘I bore her up – a scroll, a pergamen in waiting ... in wanting.’

‘No,’ Pietro says. ‘I’ll give you her insight: desire. That will unite us. I can put it on my obols.

‘Yellow is the colour of divine light. Also of gold – the metal designated by humans to denote wealth and profanity. Their convention, symbol: sheds no light, and nothing divine. Gold’s vulgar – if I could choose, I prefer lapis, or turquoise – or pearls: more lively. This doubling of significance – it’s yours, it’s earthy.... The divine, and enough cash – both unattainable....’

‘All that is your gloss, Pietro, on her philosophy,’ I say, ‘Josiane has lighted on the human pathos, put it in a nub. A stub....’

‘No, no,’ Pietro interrupts. ‘The voice is yours, Hadar. Or better – it’s your eyes. Observation. That is yours: you are the camera, the pair of goggling specs. The image: not common desire that seeks. It’s imaging, imagination. What is not, what cannot be. You have it where it cannot be, cannot be traced, for something that cannot be realised. Inside your head, shifting, sand. Magma. Want! Unfulfilment. Lack. Dissatisfaction. You expand your useless wish for Tokamak. For Doctor Chin.’

'I prefer Josiane's idea,' Clotilde says. 'Desire – not attained but unsatisfied at least. Knowing what you cannot have opens the way to second bests. Alternatives – choice, perhaps. A moderate creed, and it will do. But yours: it's devastating, Hadar.'

'Mine's devastating too,' says Josiane. 'But in a realistic kind of way.'

'Take Josiane. You have Clotilde, Hadar,' Pietro says. 'Or she has you. That's realistic too. My job is take the money in, prepare to beat the bandits off. I need aggressive sheep, Hadar. I can't manage you – that is, your errors, your imagination. Exile. A soft Dalmatian coast resort; Ovidian pipe dreams by the Black Sea – Doctor Chin, bobs up like a seal, black, rubberised. Let us imagine, with Josiane, that all will change, all will survive, the mountain or the closet opens – there stand all Bluebeard's wives, all preened and ready for the royal paradise....

'But you, Hadar! Absolutely not! Something – unspecified – something more! Not satisfaction, but the extreme of ... nothing.

'No polity survives that sort of rant ... the hope never fulfilled, a cloudy chapter from the start. Hope must be reasonable, Hadar. Here, you can be left to your own fortunes. I provide the iron cage where you can strut and flap your wings. Cages – those are up to me. The wings are yours, unless they end up in a sauce, more sour than sweet, I fear.'

*

I'm desperate. Words. They drop you in the effluent, if you're not watchful.

'Where, Pietro?' I say. 'Where do I go?'

'Far far away, like in a nursery rhyme – not like an epic, though, where you recruit a monkey army, burn me and all my retinue – fuse the glass, and there I am, eternally, the monster, trapped in a paperweight....

'When I see you, Hadar, I think "inflatable". That's what you are – and where we bonded too. My brother, my look- and think-alike. The fantasy – it makes you strong ... to carry Josiane – up and down the mountainside ... to consolidate your myth, the myth of you.... Choosing between the light, the Tokamak; and dark: Doctor Chin, the wrecks, the jellied beasts with arms – hundreds, thousands – ready for the sucker punch. Did the Doctor think these could be subjects, servants even, farmed and massacred just like the sheep up here...?

'Poor Josiane – it's clear she wants ... wants it to be different from what it always is.... That's ordinary, that's what everybody wants and will not get. That's what she got from Vanda, I would bet....'

'Where, Pietro?' I ask, I beg.

'Rest, Hadar. No climbing. Find a place with golden suns and stars, and silver grass. Maybe you could build a cart, be carried round. Or anything: a somewhere place. Write lyrics, make a fortune from your destiny.

'Be thankful the cellar here is full of ingots, or down the steps you'd go, some bored squaddie'd finish you – off! Bang bang! Off, Hadar!'

Pietro the merciful, the forgiving ... up to a point. Yellow and ruddy gleams his gold.... Clotilde, Josiane – they wring their hands, but not too hard. Selim's a trimmer – nothing to be got from him....

'Remember me, Pietro, remember me,' I say.... And as I leave, Josiane gives me used notes from her cashier's drawer.

I tell Pietro, 'You'll have a disaster – it is always so. Gold discovered, or iron converted into platinum, with a simple kit. You're ruined. And if you drop the gold, go into paper – you're always vulnerable. Remember – states are soldiers and a bank. You need guys like me to dress that up, to touch the spring of everyone's desire and fear.'

'Wise words,' says Selim, but only I can hear. 'You're not a thinker,' he goes on. 'You just look and hope, and sometimes you despair – then write it down, whatever you have thought. It's your obsession. What you did was unforgivable – at least by Pietro ... that book you cite. "The Drunken King". He took it bad.... The title! ... "and the Origin of the State..." What did you expect? You know what happens to court jesters, who hit upon the truth; the weakest spot.'

*

Farewell, Clotilde, Josiane. You join the others – another of our species problems, love and sex: brute or pansy – you leave relationships as nightmares, or as wrecks, behind.

This might be fixed? Meanwhile, those two will join the others – my stars, a chaplet glimpsed and fading: not a firmament, but enough for a constellation. Maybe – 'the "Belladonna"'.

*

Go! Go quickly.

I think more of Jung and Kubrick than of Ovid – but there is, was: Trogir. Breath of the Cathars, of Mani, the other side of good and evil, acknowledging where we were, and are. Killing pigs and suckling babies. The cathedral – home to god and devil – back to the start. Worship the powerful, and do what you can. Night-flying – that would suit.

A Dalmatian retreat: but after civil war and vandals – what might be left? Further on – the Black Sea – 'so known for its dark fogs'....

Enact the proof of what you can believe – no need to build cathedrals.

The world, my world, my destiny – my oyster, pulsating on a shell.

*

Changing nature. Doctor Chin – undergoing, mastering, all the metamorphoses, the body surprised, amazed – a new life-cycle.

Progeny. Would you recognise them? Be indifferent? ... protect ... virgin births – by the thousand. Eggs on a rock, a stick, a frond. What ambition! – millions of your children, hoovered into some vast cachelot ... making a single star is nothing in comparison: especially if you can't do it. Measnwhile, we frizzle.

Exile shows nothing – except you're off the stage. Becoming more vindictive, like Ovid. Your nature – it's your most resistant part. A kernel. Best leave it, if it isn't rotten.

Exile? Who cares? Better think always of where you are; if anybody's listening.

All over, institutions and manners are being tested. You too – the mess you've made.

More sects? More loss of faith? Poverty and luxury. Machines and messages.... All of those: and millions, milliards – your children, trying not to look edible, looking for a pilot fish, or a rock to burrow under. Flying? Dolphin chums? Or bottom feeders?

*

We were beginning to see who those old countries belonged to. Now, we start again with the one world. Whose is it? We're all exiles, all Bohemians, all inventors of ourselves.

*

The trawlers leave from this quay. Doctor Chin! I think, I cry within. Could you avoid the trawl, cut your way out? Are you the strange fish, teeth protruding, curled dead in a bucket here, a curiosity? For sale: a recipe accompanies....

'Come on my ship,' says Nisha. 'I'll give you a good time, and land you....'

'Land me like a fish?' I say. 'Is it a yacht, your boat? To Cythera? Banal eldorado for all old boys...?'

'If you like,' she says. 'Anyway, I'll book you in. We catch fish too. You're a big one – and when we have the crew – the passengers – we'll decide where you all might want to go.'

'Here, there's catastrophe,' I say. 'On board, the cry goes up – "we'll ride it out" ... That's not been my experience....'

Josiane's cash! New life, new hope – Time indeterminate again ... and I'm booked! Hooked.

'We trawl,' says Josiane. 'Bring it all up – the fish and stuff we eat; the rest – throw back.'

I shiver – maybe Doctor Chin will hear us motoring, dragging on, and find a hole....

'What we catch, is free,' she says. 'So, we've no limitations. Your voyage – it's a mystery tour. Where will we land? Who are you running from, we ask. Who'll let us dock? And Hadar – what are you on?'

'Nothing,' I say. 'I had high hopes....'

I don't mention Tokamak. For sure, they know the stars that's visible: don't steer by them – just half-remember names....

She casts us off, shouts down a pipe; we're off!

'Of course,' she says. 'It's good we're self-contained. No intimacy, of course. No hands on deck, nor in my bell-bottoms. Our travel ... could take years – but down below, there's shrouds and national flags. The states that aren't quite states – Shan State, Pietro's emirate – we don't stock flags for them: so if you die on board, a white flag does for you. And if you have fish allergies – that's just too bad.'

She scurries off into the corridors below, and laughs.

Suppose she's an inventive cook – and Doctor Chin ... skewered or stewed. We'll feast on Doctor Chin.

For the whole trip, however long – I shall not eat at all.

Nisha's small white fox sits on the rail, and hopes to snag a bird. She kills the fish caught in the trawl – precisely, with the relish of a cook, searching for consequences – the ephemeral of a digestion partly satisfied and, like a chick, mouth straining for the next....

The passengers? The crew? They're quite discreet – the crew flitter shadowy, like waiters, bell-boys; and the passengers ... they're old, they're very old.

The families send them off to cruise and die out here, it's their last treat. How they complain! And when they stop lamenting – they are dead.

I look for cabins where they languish: instead, there's a space, a hold, set out with beds, quite primitive, the bedsteads like a military hospital's, chipped white enamel, bedpans: the ancients moribund, pass nothing on, no stories, not even viruses.

'This is a ship of death, Nisha,' I say.

'We're on the sea,' she says. 'The sea is nowhere, so you get the taste of not existing, not being anywhere at all, not able to get off or to arrive, not going back, your story is exactly the same as everybody's. If you start to ramble on – someone will interrupt and ramble on....

'You must be strong,' I say. 'To spend your life with people who will die, and maybe catch it from them for yourself....'

She weeps, she hugs me, and I feel her body, bones – bundles of sticks wrapped in a canvas. 'I have the faith,' she says, 'that one day we shall land, the fox will race upon the sand, the nights will pass without a star, the sun will set without evoking pink and purple passions, the engorgement of the whole....

'They follow us, we follow them,' she goes on, again the cicerone. 'The radios, the voices, tongues of everywhere. We cannot land without permission, and there's no one, no one alive, who wants our company....'

'Our wisdom....' I join in.

'Well,' says Nisha. 'You must know: no one will understand us. The radio speaks a thousand dialects, and here on board – you, Hadar, are not passenger nor crew. You seek a refuge, but it's contradictory, you want a refuge without danger – a home, that is, lost long ago, your safety ... it's unreachable, for ever a horizon, a mirage always there and seeming real upon the sea ... receding and untouchable.'

'This melancholy, Nisha.... The shepherds – they would shout, blow horns that resonate from valley to the crest,' I say. 'They rant like Robinsons, and rage and curse – but here – to shout is useless, even to pipe is like the wind in shrouds: the ropes – shrouds, Nisha?'

'That's what we call them, Hadar,' Nisha says. 'Shrouds. It's what they are. You hear the crack of sails we haven't got, the creaking of a wooden hull long past been eaten by the worms ... we walk the planks all day, we are old salts, the salt corrodes our plates.... *Mattanze,* Hadar – a massacre of all that lives beneath our keel. We have no time, just space without an energy ... so – I mete out time and extinction on all that swims or drifts or clings....'

She weeps desperately – I cling to her as drowning sailors cling to lobster pots, a bell-buoy, an automatic light upon a reef....

*

The wine-dark sea...?

'Yes, yes,' she says, 'I have a bottle in my bunk....' And so we go and drink, drink deep....

'A distant relative? Hitler's lover: is that your history, Nisha dear?' I ask.

'All relatives are distant: that's why they're relative,' she says. 'Lover, victim, reluctant ally.... We're all in the same boat now. See my hands – it won't wash off, the blood, but we must eat, go on and on. One day – we'll reach the island, where no one tells us to fuck off and find another haven.'

We drink, we cuddle, we throw up, we lurch and stagger. The sea – its special sickness....

Nisha says: 'You're nothing, Hadar, a pure soul. You're evanescent, one who searches, but it's you that's lost. Maybe you have a skeletom. Someone you met by night, locked up. You're innocent, a Bluebeard, no feelings, no regrets. *Alles leben.* You're an innocent, forever guilty: kidnapping of everyone for your enjoyment, yours alone. All locked away: – and you know where. You make the miracle – now you see them, now ... and there they are! The women and the men! Victory in space, victory in the depths – unlikely, and impossible; never, never, not ever ... but on you go, like the ship – the sea, the ship, it never ends. You do. You think you won't. You end, Hadar! The ship goes on.'

'It goes on for everyone,' I say. It's weak.

'You're drunk, Nisha,' I say.

'It's a drunken ship,' she says.

The motor stops, the motion – it goes on. 'I could slip,' she says, 'over the side. As an experiment. You're a heavy load, Hadar. All this crew is. Dead weights, a ballast, bilge. Any excuse serves me. To get away.'

'I'd help you, Nisha,' I say, 'but if you are not there, overboard – how can I?'

'That's all I need,' she says. 'You not being there. Hurrah! Let's hear a shanty, jolly tars! No melancholy.'

'They turn the engine low at night,' I say. 'We still pulse forward, but we are becalmed – we sail on. We have no sails. I think we stop over the deepest place – a rift, a trench, where life starts and never moves. The filaments of life mark time, and nothing moves, no one has hands, no one will wind – and no one ticks or tocks.'

'You're drunker than I am, Hadar,' Nisha says. 'Though how can anybody say, tell, the degrees of being drunk? Homicide, betrayal, or just too clever, by a half? A half knot, a twist of the garotte, and all your friends to see you off.'

'Yes, my great friend, Pietro,' I say. 'He'll do well until he trips, and I'll fall with him, though no one remembers me, remembers what I did back then. Wanting: that was my discovery. Imagine – eternal Columbus Day. Everyone discovering New York – give it a new name, bury what the natives called it: hell or home.'

'We'll find a rock, a stretch of sand,' says Nisha. 'You can name it, even after you. Then I'll discover it, and change the name. And – if you want America – we can't. It's behind us. You should be glad.'

'Almost all the countries are behind us,' I say. 'The big ones; the little ones encysted in the mountains. The big ones caught us; they were seaweed. Russia was the Sargasso, a sea without land boundaries; America invented plastic and Greek fire: burned, and then marooned itself in rainbow shoals.

'We're free, it's all open sea. We can eat our way now, so long as there are fish. From below, we must look reassuring – like a turtle or a whale – powering along, and clicking rhymes. Poetry? Whale rap? Going somewhere – to copulate, meet friends and schmooze ... exhale some foam, and have a glass of plankton....'

'Yes,' she says. 'I've another bottle of plankton here, that needs seeing to....'

*

In the morning – a mound of moribund flappers, twitchers – a battalion of sword-fish, armed and drowning, suffocating – quick! quick! Kill them all, Nisha ... and she does.

'Salt them, Nisha,' I say. 'Salt's all around. Hang them from the spars, like linen handkerchiefs....'

Nisha is driven – Vanda too, until it ran out, the drive, and she was ordinary. Nisha's fate as well: exhaustion.

'I can be your guide,' she says, pausing, shouldering her spike.

'We're nowhere, Nisha,' I say.

'I'll show you over; the boat,' she says. 'It's all we have, unless we slide below. Over the side.'

'There will be land,' I say. 'Even beneath the sea – there's land. An island? A pumice rock that comes and goes.'

'This is an island,' Nisha says. 'The boat,' taking my hand and pulling us along cream corridors – 'Wet Paint' it says on everything, the handles on the doors, the bulkheads, then the holds, the dying ancients.... 'We bank their pensions,' Nisha says. 'The log. There is a powerful log, our King – we falsify the dates, we tax, inherit, we'll be rich when all around are far below our keel....'

'I've been a vagabond,' I say. 'And a prophet: once in direct discourse with a God, and now He's gone – I'm connected only to a happenstance, to fortune, whose impotence is very much like God's....'

We laugh. Our hangovers – they dissipate on several tots of rum. 'Not rum,' says Nisha. 'It's early for that. It's grog, medicinal.'

And so it is.

*

'Nisha, there's always land,' I say, frustrated, hungry. 'Or else all maps would be solid blue. Even the sky is blue except, depending on the hour, it's black.'

'I'll ask the helmsman,' Nisha says. 'Though he stands at the back ... I never figured out how he knows where to go, or how we don't hit land....'

'A bird,' I say, impatiently. 'They get sent off –'

'What do they know?' asks Nisha. 'Fox can smell blood and bones – he knows the news before it's made.'

The little murderous beast perks up, pretends to follow our discourse

'Land is land,' says Nisha, holding on to me. 'You need a special type. You're an Olympian: a pygmy polity – would drag....'

'I don't discriminate,' I say. 'The ship has emptied out. No Doctor Chin swarmed up the netting on the sides....'

'You have to learn the names of things on ships – or else you'll have bad luck – even worse, and worser still,' and Nisha laughs, 'You'll sink the lot of us on board.'

*

Unto an isle so long unknown....

Andrew Marvell

'I stake my life on this landfall,' I tell Nisha.

Of course if you are at sea, land is elusive – it's a challenge to get there, anywhere, and to find the suitable. But for many years – it's been done. Many fail and disappear – most, many, manage to get somewhere that they want, or find by long settlemement that – it's tolerable. I don't mean that Nisha is a liar, or a deceiver. It's as if she has said – to herself, to the crew, so discreet, so uncensorious, so complicit – 'You think you're smart, living with serious people, their projects that are radical and fail. A journey – you arrive, get off the carrier – and there you are! My idea is different, even a little mad. Now – let's see if you can get the better of me – in a vessel whose parts resemble what you've known on land, floors, doors ... but here – the terms are different, carry good luck, bad luck, as if you're in the forest of indigenes, deciding what to kill and eat.

Are we again, with Nisha – 'lost', as in the experiment apparently devised for Doctor Chin, who I still love, still feel the frisson of our skins – the oilskins ... the narrow bunk, the confidences and the whispering – all vanished with a plunge, the Doctor, unseen by me, no word, no farewell hug or kiss or promise ... over the side, all guttapercha, glassed in, unrecognisable, a space warrior in armour – against all convention, down – instead of up...? A warrior, slicing into waves.... And now Nisha: no 'where shall we go?', no 'where do you want to pass your exile?' or a voyage terminating, motivated somehow, even if only for the benefits – health, culture, sea breeze, the company at captain's table, or piped up and down the stairs, gangways – piped like trees of exotic birds, onward and upward to the crest, fly or clamber and – there! the ocean! But – land. Land ho!

That's our home, that's where we nest and clack our beaks.

The sea! It seems a different world. There must be a frame to frame the picture. Land frames the sea that lies beneath, ahead, behind. Pictures without frames – those are unbounded, they're the real, the material, the world without its culture, its art ...They are its everyday, its ordinariness. Land frames, gives proportion to the incontentinental ocean, infinite, without a boundary, unrestrained ... without a sense, a soul. What fills in the space between the lands....

'Trust me!' Nisha says. 'You must be very very careful where you land. There's slavery, conscription, penury –

every land has those, and maybe what you seek does not exist. Trust me to find what may not quite exist, not yet, just like your Tokamak, or the Doctor's realm of undersea – both seriously sought: the energy, the everlasting food ... so near, but occulted, some twist, some apparatus lacking – leaving hope abandoned....

'I don't give hope, I massage expectation….'

Alcine and Bonnie – not at all opaque. Pietro's polity – transparent: you give submission, service and your life: he gives a motivation; daily pay, protection. Unequal exchange, of course, for he is strong and you are weak, and nothing can redress your being born, or made, subordinate. Ductile. An apparatus for the magnifiying, the magnificence – of Pietro ... who shivers every night, thinking of his fate – the knife, the bomb, or the garotte....

'Try holding a straight line,' I say. 'Nisha! That way, we'll hit a land, even an island....'

'That's what landsmen think,' she says. 'Leave it to me. You'd have us on the rocks.'

'I'm confused,' I say. 'Is it a game, a puzzle, a test? Do you want me to stay with you? I'm the one in trouble, I need a place. You've made a labyrinth, waves instead of hedges, walls.

'I'm an exile, a criminal, a victim of bad luck ... I beg you, Nisha – let me find peace. Help me get out the web.'

'A game?' she says. 'I don't think so. You're a passenger. Sit – we do the steering: we try to make a friendly context ... clean sheets...'

'If I learn the words: capstan bars. Marlin spikes. Could I choose a route....' I shout.

'Set a course, it's called,' she says. 'Learning a language takes a lifetime, not to mention the practice after. And steering round false friends....'

She throws a canvas bucket over the side, fills it with water, hoists it back up, throws the water into the scuppers, approving of the transient cleanliness.

'I could never do that,' I say.

'You observe, Hadar,' she says. 'You flit, and it looks as if you move from something promising to something else. I contemplate. Don't budge. It's the only way of living in this vast water. When you're in orbit, look down, it's tiny, though. A splodge.'

I say, '"Wanting" was my discovery. I want to get off. This is not at all what I meant. You don't try to fit me in.'

'That's not in the cruise,' she says. 'Read the ticket. Want is satisfied – there's no more, no "wanting". It's all guaranteed. Choose ordinariness – it's hard, but not as hard as other things.'

True. Vanda wanted, wanted everything, all sides to win. Nothing. You get nothing.

Doctor Chin – that's hard. The test. Really hard.

*

Land. Land crystallising through the fog. Long painted boats, thin as bean pods, mustered. Paddlers. Could be Senegal? The fox jumps down, and swims – climbs aboard a pirogue, stands, silver-white at the prow. He's found his craft, his berth. The idiot – a life again against nature.

No Nisha, no Sparks; the captain, if there's one, sleeping deep below. The ship – Moored or grounded? Hard to tell. I climb down a rope, and run, run up the beach.

There's people standing round: There's slaves and slavers, people cruising, people going to New York and fleeing it. There's people refugees, prisoners escaping, people with faith, people with regrets. Sick and hungry, lovers and unloved. Guys in uniform, guys whose pants are falling off.

'What are we waiting for?' I ask. The impetus of landing, running – has died away; I'm lurching, sliding, holding on, being brushed away....

'It's to be administered,' he says. 'Put into our categories. Snapped and printed. Declare what we want to be: preferred height and weight ... people we know, sex performed, militancies, wars fought, famines experienced, last time in tents ... under the stars ... regrets. Other places we would much more like to be. Oaths of loyalty. Banks and jails. You fill the form, they give you points for neatness. Then they question you ... quite differently....'

'And then?' I ask. 'Give us money, extradite us ... give us guns or take them from us...?

'There's resources,' says the guy – Kadr. 'They divide those by the new arrivals. If there's space and food – it's mostly breadfruit: you can stay.'

'If not?' I ask.

'Then it's the same, you stay. You're not viable, is all. Don't expect much, and don't steal,' Kadr says. 'This is a good place. They don't want you, don't ask for love of country – and you don't give it. You'll want to leave, but there's no way. Things run aground.... Not to be counted on.' He looks anxiously at our beached ship.

'I'm the last,' I say. 'The rest are dead. Or puzzling. The service is good, satisfying. The food repels. The tickets cost, but you don't go anywhere.'

'You're lucky,' Kadr says. 'Not to be signed on as crew. Or – stowing a cargo of turkey birds! Those are greedy, loud – they get alarmed and rock the boat, you have to calm them. At Thanksgiving, there's a massacre – I don't give thanks for anything ... it's not appropriate.'

'You're at one with me,' I say, thankful to have found this tall Masai, his knees like knobs on knobkerries: leaping up lemur-like to have his head brush the foliage ... the reassurance of being tall....

'Tell me how to survive here,' I say, 'and I'll tell you about Tokamak.'

'Stick close to me,' he says, squeezing my shoulder, 'Forget about Tokamak.'

I think – this is the perfect place to mention 'wanting' – for sure, I'd have a herd of acolytes. Best stay schtum, though. 'Wanting' is dynamite. This is a small, fragile place....

*

The compound's tough. Might Nisha work this holding pen, selling her tickets?

I could go back – or forward – with her.... 'Friendly service' – that was the offer, 'Any destination considered'.

All considered, none confessed and none chosen or attained. Ha! The island – the continent – it rocks. 'There's divers underneath,' says Kadr. 'Trying to underpin – we have to rush from side to side to balance out, we run, we grunt and squeal, terrified the land will break away from land, and drift us out to sea....'

And Doctor Chin – maybe below, with stanchions, a pneumatic jack – bolting us to pumice or to basalt – thinking 'This must, this will, end, end very bad.... We have to find a way to coexist – air, water – and the fire at the core, fire almost hot enough to be a sun, a star, already it has passed the procedure similar to Tokamak, however banal – a huge gas fire, to power the microwave, let us sneak down and watch Deadpool at dead of sleepless night.'

'You viscid men,' says Kadr, taking his hand away from me and wiping it on his penis-sheath – 'came from the sea. Your uncles – cucumbers, your aunties – spiders. We're the only ones who came from stardust – from the black of distance, dry and swift....'

I scoff: 'Peanuts, Kadr: my dear friend Vanda – she packed your product. Nuts. Forget the firmament – think snacks and plantations ... that is your orbit, the cycle ... sit in the saddle and pedal, Kadr.' I laugh. He laughs.

'You're an Olympian, Hadar,' he says. 'A true philosopher! Your thigh boots – blood and scales! Fins in your beard, and the stench! And you're in my team, I'm your shift boss....'

We active ones – there's team sports, and throwing sticks, and javelins, and baskets on your wrists to throw clay balls. And we produce – wooden stuff. If you shout, you're heard on the other side of the island. All the teams are mixed, by law. What is mixed? It's not hard to imagine – we're all here, washing in from everywhere: all wondering who'll win and lose.

'I guess you were bad, Hadar,' says Kadr. 'Or lost. Or stupid good – maybe you couldn't concentrate, judge yourself. Well, here there's no facility to judge you. Keep it cool: the big things will come, land on your head, and you'll be tested, but believe me, not judged.'

'It's aimless,' I say. 'It's improvised. I come from the top places. Cash. Intrigue. Landscape. Dams ten times Itaipu: keeping going in a big world.'

'And how did you do, Hadar?' Kadr asks. 'Screwing like a rat, I bet! Salty! Sargassum accessories in your underpants. You tricky matelot! I bet those cats frolicked round your sublime fishiness!'

*

And on he parleys. He's a great guzlar, and the guys in the squad gather round, and on he rhymes, takes out a kemanche from somewhere, and he sits and yarns, plays and makes up satires: on me, on what he thinks, fantasises what I might have done, but doesn't mention the murder and the exile, as if those are connected with anything or anyone except with me....

'Pussy's pieces,' says a guy, Mehmet, his long white clothes quite stained, his hennaed beard a straggle ... there's a guffaw, and on he goes, 'We're dross,' he says, 'And we're indifferent. This is a great place to be – for two days. We've been here for years – they didn't want to take us in, and no one wants to take us off....'

I dump my boots, comb the fish-scales from my hair with salt-cracked fingers – my body's striped red and white with scars: tumbling on those basalt rocks. I remember Josiane, and weep. I remember Clotilde – and I sob.

The women here – their nature's changed. They're bigger, more aggressive than the men, stronger too, better at games, and much more generous ... victory, defeat – who cares? They've gone like parakeets – the females bigger, less coloured than the males: the males eat less, try to defend the nests, grow small and smaller still ... get bullied too....

'It's like the future here,' says Agit. 'And it's like the past. If you think it is the present – you'd despair.'

*

'These boats,' says Kadr, pointing to the rows of red-blue-green pirogues outrigged and leaking – the hopeful Fox.... 'Won't face the waves. Our friend,' and he points to the Fox, waiting for something to move.... 'Is wasting time.'

'The women – they're all engineers,' says Mehmet, hopping up and down. 'They'll build a proper ship. I'm sure they'll take us off.'

'Oh,' I say, tormented by my hope, my fear that we'll be here eternally. 'Yes! They're noble souls, they will provide where need is great. Bless them, each one, their power, their benevolence.... But the material – here it's rocks, sand and saplings....'

'It's new technology,' says Kadr. 'A mine of aluminium – you fold the paper, the foil – a ship-shape comes quite natural – and off, with caution – off you go! All of us too, for sure.'

'That's nonsense,' Agit says. 'They'll take one male, and if they want, they'll milk him, like ants milk aphids ... if they want some kids, that is. The rest of us – stay here!'

Compassion and passion – there's hormones ... without the fire, must the fellow-feeling wane? Perhaps – the men here, unkempt and childish, are just unappetising. Poor specimens, a bit louche.... I wonder, missing the boat?... Men – Man – speaking a language not much more refined 'than rooks or monkeys' – maybe, maybe, one wonders....

*

> *... must we return again to the forests to live among bears?* J-J. Rousseau, *A Discourse on the Origin of Inequality*

'No forests here,' says Kadr: 'If there were, I'd show you how to build a galleon.'

*

I think – even Nisha, the endless journey, without purpose, without love, without companionship, wave after wave – and yet.... And yet, one moves ... the scenery changes, so do you....

She said, 'Hadar, when you need me, I shan't be there. You know, it's terribly hard to leave a person. It's easy, terribly easy, to leave your ideas, convictions. But people stick, like the skin on a banana. You peel one, throw it away, then you see – a forest of them, all the same, you'd never have the time to peel each one ... to find the fruit, what you can consume: so, you must eliminate ... the skins....'

'But they're all different, Nisha,' I said. 'Skins' – that's what doctor Chin had said, almost. My love, the Doctor: to pass exams, you must speak Party, follow the thought. Mao and Xi Jinping. To be a Mandarin, you must know Mandarin, but all the same, you're still a Mandarin....

'You're wrong,' said Nisha. 'It's not the bananas. It's you that's different. The bananas are all the same, identical, there is no end to them.'

It's a mystery, but all the same – I need Nisha now. And her ship....

'We could fight them,' Agit says. 'To get on their boat.'

'No use,' says Mehmet. 'There's more of them, and stronger.... And – it isn't seemly....'

*

They're scientists, so a foil boat's quite practicable. The females' nature's changed; perhaps just it's surfaced, been asserted. No need to take the radical turn, to change the nature of humanity, of everyone. No need to dive, follow Doctor Chin, who's anyway – gone where?

I despair.

'We're sea-birds,' Kadr says. 'Carried here and there by wind or wave. When we don't eat – we skirl. We land to copulate – and then we're off – distances no ship could contemplate – circling over Mecca, over the Dead Sea, like lost bombers, disarmed, wing-weary, then away, away....'

'And here we are,' says Mehmet, sadly. 'No one knows where, and if they knew, they would not care. God knows. But we don't believe in Him, and nor do you, Hadar, though you're a son of Abraham....'

'We all are that, Mehmet,' I say. 'Much good does it do!'

*

We stand on the shore, unmoving in our stained white clothes, and watch the foil boat start to force its way through the breakers and their spume. The craft wavers, reaches the swell, the women thrust their flimsy paddles deep in the green waters – the metal of their craft dartles gold and silver, and we hear their slender high ancient voices, like the choirs at Zagorsk, sing out sweet and defiant.

'You, Hadar,' Kadr says, near to tears. 'Suffer ... you're an observer, and there's nothing to observe. I'm an inventor, I make, devise – and I can't get out, there's no materials, it's all inert. We can't make anything of us two, we do not match, we do not complement.'

'They'll send for us,' says Mehmet in hope.

'We didn't ask them to,' says Kadr: 'Why should they?'

*

It can't end here.

Maybe Doctor Chin is lost – another sacrifice to science, or to fantasy. Tokamak ... some day, perhaps, when it's too late. And Pietro – small dictatorships – they seemed most likely to endure – they are boutiques, luxurious feeding places – niches for exotic birds.... Who cares about the executions behind the shed at night? No one here does – we'd most of us enjoy a trial, a change of menu, petitions for reprieve – even the chop that clean and neat concludes the inconclusive. But – it's never so. We're lost, abandoned here, like when the motor stopped at sea....

My lovers.... Always round their heads, like gnats – circling Eros, Tyche, and their friend, dear Thanatos. Did anyone want me? Or was it only me, who wanted...?

'Hurry!' Kadr shouts. 'There's scraps of foil been left behind: no cruiser, nor a frigate even – but coracles! One for each pirate, each adventurer!'

These silver rounds – saucers not for the brave: for the impatient. Use your hands as your paddles, just wait for the wind that blows off the shore....

'Farewell, farewell!' the faint-hearts shout – and off we spin – the wind stiffens, sends us out, further, further, rotating, buckling, the foil distorts ... we're low in troughs, labouring, our arms flail, try to set us on a course – we lose sight of anything but waves.

Kadr gave no hope, no destination.

'If they see you, they may pick you up,' he shouts, 'Who, who?' we shout back, our wind against the wind ... Mehmet already tires, the sea sucks like a sink, he's in a twist, down down he goes – he prays. That's right. All you can do – and Agit finds a crest and rides it, his nest a wheel, a dime on a wire....

'If you can't go on, go back,' I think it's Kadr's voice: it's quite impossible, forward or back, the wind is cheeky, then malign, then intent on driving us – flightless chicks in shining nests ... over and over the edge, a fall and rise of water, drop bounce and fall again....

THE END

Kadr has gone.

I think of Fox, pointing, bewildered, fixed on his prow, waiting for: adventure? safety? for Nisha, her lumbering ship?

Doctor Chin said, before the plunge: 'I'm a communist, so I love to be free .... I don't denounce; I don't believe in machines, social credit for being good and right – or registering eyes ... my iris is my flower.... Beneath the waves – no one knows who I am ... eyes open or shut, no one sees. That's freedom, Hadar....'

And I think – the experiment, living under the sea, changing your shape, your species ... it's drastic: effacement, you'd say – self-destruction, concealment. Elimination.

Even – it was the forte of the Doctor: altruism, the celebrated altruistic suicide. And if Doctor Chin – maybe all the rest? Professor Hoover too – over the side, an end, end to it all, an abnegation. Pietro and me – sent off in our squalor, our inflatable, to live; the unworthy ones, manumitted, selfish, the self-indulgent. Surviving, lost, cast-offs and castaways.

*

Is that the fluke of a whale or the shape of a ship...?

Giant tables, lit up and deserted.... Things not belonging – tumble and gyre....

Nisha

Nisha?

*

I rise from the sea – my white dishdasha whiter than it's ever been – shines with my revelation ...

*

No experiment! That expedition, all those sages; Adil the faithful, the equitable, him as well. All overboard ... a sect, off to meet the nothingness they all believed in. Hand in hand, changing their essence, scientists into fish, the living into the dead.

Surrender? Despair?

*

And my enquiries – how modernity changed our personality, our goals, beliefs ... the failure of the Tokamak, the mastery of the firmament.... All written down and filed. Then came in machines, intelligences alien and artificial. I ponder this. My thought, observation – all wasted, superannuated.

*

I have no shoes – they'd have pierced the bottom of my boat. Think, think into my new reality.

The beach is pebbles, so I hop, pick up a stem of kelp, and like a salted prophet, labour up the shingle: I'm salted ... like a peanut! and I laugh. Vanda! Who remembers her? Salting, roasting, packing....

Prosperity has come while I was Crusoefied, on my island, on Nisha's ship. Capital has landed here.

But – all my mates ... lost in sea. Alas, Kadr, my brother....

The buildings – in my absence, they've grown up like hemlocks, cow parsley – tall, tall, their shadows throw dark stubbles on the streets. Names that you know ... chocolates and underwear.

Look for the poverty – down the alleyways, there's almost everyone! And here's Selim! A spot where he, the destitute, plods on. He doesn't move, cramp, crosslegged. A good pitch, this, covers the sidewalk....

'Selim!' I shout, and throw aside my seaweed prop, embrace. He hasn't recognised me, but still.... Humanity! The touch of skin.... He sells, he waits, what patience he's acquired!

Batteries – re-charged, re-hab chargers, for motors, or your little telephone. Cables for jump starts, though he's not going anywhere.

Poor speaks to poor and sells to poor. It's still the world I left....

I must see Pietro, my old friend.... But now, how many friends there'll be! A line as long as this whole place, all on their knees, all trying to evolve a tale ... extort some gift....

'Selim!' I say. 'It's Hadar – you remember, the exile, the murderer, the ideologue without a pal.... Surely you remember...?'

He shies away. Maybe I'm too honest with my faults....

I tell him everything.

'Pietro?' he explains. 'He's protected now.... The crew's depleted. Those we knew – the cashiers – are cashiered. Clotilde, Josiane – gone, blown away, over the rocks. He rules, he doesn't bank. He sits – a toad. Then leaps in splendour with his toadies.... A bodyguard. They parade – a company, battalion.... All he sees is armed men now.

'What do you bring, Hadar? Not prophesy, I hope. We've thousands like you, they don't get in the door.'

'No first ladies, then?' I ask.

'You are a threat, Hadar,' says Selim. 'Don't go, dressed and bearded as you are, up to the palace – you'll be shot. And think, think with great care. Do you want a favour from him, from the chief? You could set out something useful on the sidewalk – not near me, though! – and show you're honest, striving, tied in to the economy, the ethic too.

'Go to the palace – and you're at a risk. Big favours mean big sacrifices. What you're asked to do is more than what you'd get from him.... That is the way.... Now I remember – how you talk of friends who don't reciprocate when you ask so much of them. They give, and then there's nothing left ... for them, and nothing new from you.

'Old shoes, Hadar – here, they fetch a fortune, if you have a source....'

'Wise words, Selim,' I say. 'That advice is worth a life. I could choose a spot in the next alley – in the shade? It's cold.

In the sun? You roast. Old shoes – you improvise a sole, over the hole it goes, you glue – and it'll last you ... I have been chosen – to survive. Not, it seems, chosen to observe. I sell used stuff, like all the rest. It works that way.'

The end: only the sea starts up eternally – 'the sea, the sea always begun again....'

*

I join the line: Pietro's palace – pink, like a wedding cake. One statue on the top – it's him, in bearskin – a tiara? shapka? golden helm? He sparkles in the sun. It's very hot – the line sits down and rests against the railings.

Too late, I remember – I'm an exile, permanently. Here I am, though: shall I be recognised? They search us, places where you wouldn't put a stick of dynamite ... perfume us, give us each a clean dishdasha. One by one....

He's behind glass, blue-tinged, as if he's Neptune, or in a tank, alone.

The label on me says 'Kadr'.

'You're a naughty boy, Hadar,' he says. 'My! How you've aged; repented, possibly. And do you want as much as once you did?'

'Peace, Pietro,' I say. 'Grant me peace.'

'And Doctor Chin?' he asks. 'That was some love! I find with China you do deals, but best at arm's length – you were trusting. Doctor Chin, though, just disappeared....'

'A noble soul,' I say. 'Tormented too – but what we didn't realise....'

‘Was,’ Pietro interrupts. ‘That shipwrecks make your fortune. Mine. In your case, Hadar: – not! It’s the sea again for you, I fear. If it was up to me....’ and he lifts up my dishdasha with a long stick. Scars and salt-cracks.... He laughs, ‘Yes, you’ve metamorphosed, my dear. You’re shrivelled right away! The problem for me, and now you, is: I can’t pardon you. I am not what you see. Behind my throne there is a force.... I’m sponsored. It’s the economy.... Sometimes it falls, crashes, disappears – and so you need insurers.’

‘But that’s you!’ I say. ‘You are the bank. The bank insures the bank.’

‘Hm, yes,’ he says. ‘A bolshie mode of thought.... That’s right. But as I said – I’m not me, not just a raggedy old crow that sits on what is yours, gained well or really bad. Of course – your money’s mine, it’s my, it’s our, security; but if I invest real bad, I need insurance so I don’t lose it all – and remember, dear – it’s yours! You don’t want that ... a bankruptcy....’

‘I know,’ I say. ‘Don’t let’s discuss! Why do your sponsors want to send me off again? No profit to them: and as you see: I’m cracked and scarred....’

‘It was the wanting, Hadar,’ Pietro says. ‘Your downfall. We all want. It’s when there are catastrophes that follow like the clouds that course, parade, for ever: until one day – there’s nothing. Never more.... No future we can want. What we all “want” now – is – “Stop!” No more a fall, then up and off again. We want it all to stop – now, where we were miserable, maybe, but living, hoping, I feel it too. Dancing naked round the fire, Clotilde and Josiane in tow – those were the nights I'd want again, to study, savour: ... my Sunset Boulevard....

'Your message, Hadar, starts progressive – but, with catastrophes – it turns right back. You're an old Tory now. That's bad, discouraging. What next? Could my throne fall? My guys, my band of boosters – turn against me?

'You've seen too much – and now, too much of you's a venom ... an emetic, purge....'

'We didn't realise,' I say. 'What that experiment at sea, what it was to be. They all followed Doctor Chin. Over the side. A suicide. Lemmings.... *Assez connu....*'

'An excess of taking a responsibility:' Pietro says: 'They make disasters, but there they are, round the back – tinkering and counselling, trying to wipe up the mess. There's makers of the bomb, and "physicists concerned", seeking the third way everybody talks about. Then – the lightbulb! The big answer! – do yourself in, so's there's no question of your complicity or big mistakes..... I often thought it odd, that we were saved. Us knowing, deserving, least of all....

'It turned out well for me, and bad for you, Hadar. Who knows – your turn will come, perhaps. But – just not here.'

'Mercy, Pietro. It doesn't cost,' I say. 'No one will know. It mustn't be for show – not like your act, the prancing and the throne-room, the bodyguard.... "Pardon," you say, discrete.'

'These pralines,' Pietro interrupts. 'They send them: try one. Nay, have a poke!' He grins and winks.

He presses it into my hand. 'You know the fable, Hadar,' Pietro says. 'The guy says to the snake – "don't bite me", the snake just tilts its head, suffocates him in its coils and swallows him.'

*

'Look!' he says. 'My video! There's the boyars and the crowd – "long life, glory – our little father...."'

'I love the bells,' I say. 'You need your feet in the loop to get the effect of joy and panic....'

'See – the tributes,' Pietro insists. 'These are my backers....'

Scurrying along, guys in blue suits, blue ties.

'I can't disappoint my fans,' he says. 'Although the business isn't in my hands....'

'I hear the cashiers went,' I say.

'I didn't do exams,' he says. 'I just know how it's done. That's not enough. It never has been. I'm the clown. The dancing clown.'

He weeps. 'The grave, Hadar,' he says. 'Beckons. It yawns – it must be tired – seeing us in millions, marching macho up the avenue, then down into the sod. Imagining our tamgas – defaced: our brands modified, the camels marked anew....'

'Come, Pietro,' I say. 'That's long ago. No one cares now. Death moves among us unhindered. We've done nothing for anyone to mourn that we, that anyone, can't do it over....'

'Wisdom, Hadar,' Pietro says. 'They say wise words are prophesies of fools: mocked. Unheeded.'

'You've lost it, Pietro,' I tell him: 'Your pizzaz. Let's sneak out, pop a pill and neck some beers....'

'They'd recognise me....' he says, drawing back, then – pushing ahead....

He's scampering towards the back, running, dodging his minders – they're scanning porn or playing cards, and out we go – 'A spree!' he shouts.

I'd forgotten he is small, round, hairy, long rubbery arms. Ridiculous, perhaps.

Are his sponsors creating the ridiculous, I ask myself. It seems the contrary of what they ought to want – but that might be the unintended consequence, a consequence that leads us to a source. The source is not ridiculous, it's the obsession. The banality of hunger, the need to plant more, and more to avoid catastrophe, and then to stack a surplus, for the winter, for spring sowing.... There's something of the squirrel or the fox in most ... you wouldn't say it was ridiculous, but maybe it looks silly or quite horrible ... the rite of spring, a sacrifice that's solemn, that glues the group, a mystic union that's quite misplaced and unavailing. A waste ... that leads to Pietro, banking clown, master of his revels. Ridiculous – integral to the human cycle....

He's hopped down from the throne and skittered out the back. No one is interested. We roister down an alleyway, there's low bars and high jinks, bottles and tarts, house specialities.... 'Let's find Selim,' Pietro shouts.... 'Clotilde and Josiane....'

Selim's scared and busy. Sends us away.

Pietro says to me, 'I may look a freak, talk like a hyena, but you, Hadar, you always backed off the topmost spot. Being clever's nothing. Being a critic's pitiful. I went for it, and got it. If what it is is rubbish – I got there, I'm still there. You got wet feet.'

We're drunk, but not aggressive. Insulting, but taking it, riposting well....

There's women in the bars, they stare at us, don't bother, we can't start anything, anything at all.

'Exile,' Pietro says. 'You couldn't metaphorise it properly, my friend. Just suffered. Even getting there, to the Ovidian place: it could have killed you. No stature drawn up from the pain.... Any idiot can suffer: every idiot does. Suffering's what idiots do.'

We keep changing bars. People stare at us. We're very drunk and mouthy now.

'Do you have lookalikes?' I ask him. They all do. Maybe he's not Pietro even, not even Pietro drunk. Someone paid to look like him, because – he looks like him, and vice versa.

This is no fun.

He says, 'If you want justice, Hadar, you will need a lawyer. You must go through the courts.'

'No, I don't want all that fuckabout,' I say.

'You must!' he says, putting his mouth into my ear. 'It may take years. They may say no – it's worse than being tried, and they may find out....'

'No ship!' I shout.

Pietro's bored – he leaves my case. 'I do what I want,' he shouts. 'I'm beastly: king of the beasts.'

'And I'm the lion of Judah,' I shout back. 'Cutting people free....'

He goes quite sober – 'That's your problem, Hadar. Inconsistency. You want the world, and yet it's all about some lover of the month who won't do what you want, be what you think you want. You put together those two things, idiotic and fantastic. Philosophy and gender. Want and sex. That's what you call your star. More useless than another Tokamak.'

It's true. So what? That's what I am.

If you observe, you don't need to be lovable.

*

'Your friend,' the barman says. 'May need your help.'

He does. He's got his foot stuck in a hole. Those Turkish-type stand-up bogs – hygienic, but their slope is slippery. He doesn't need to ask for help – he fills the space that everybody needs.

'Get me out!'

There's guys with saws, wise words, and grease.

I'm drunk. So what? I have been drunk before.

No ship, I think. What then? The mountains! On the rocks. A shepherd with no sheep. Up high, you look down on two valleys, two different ways of being.... Pietro's, and the peanut factory. There'll be no waves, no fish, no moving parts with names to learn. Up, up and away....

*

When you've drink taken, is the best time to climb. Higher and higher – you fall and bleed, your blood doesn't sting, it could be someone else's. Down the other side, there will be Vanda. She's ordinary. What happened to Shan State?

Ordinary too? Clotilde and Josiane – they'll have moved on. Another bank?

I shout out names: Koselleck! Wedekind!

Who shouts mine?

The future? Consequences? The suffering? No one answers, no one awakes, no shepherd without sheep bursts from his hut to embrace or threaten...

My life, embroidered like a quilt with names familiar but hard to place, unique, the centre of a little transitory world, balances upon these sharp black rocks. Whoops! Up, up,up! I am a drunken goat, escaping from the sacrificial table.

My star – still up among the millions. If you could make a compact ceiling of them, it would glow, faint. Abundance of Tokamaks, flaming useless weakly on and on and on through their excessively long lives.

Higher and higher – Pietro's palace, pink-stuccoed, dwindles to a pimple.

No peanut factory – there's 'biopharmaceuticals' instead.

It's packing stuff in bags and tubes.

WISDOM

THE FOREST'S full of poachers, bandits – so, the tiny house I rent there – more of a hut – is protected; disproportionately for the poverty within. There's a wooden door, guarded by a metal gate with bars, only a half. A space between the gate and door. It's cold, and cats want to get in, in to the warm. They're wrong, it isn't warm inside. I often find one or two, waiting. Today, there's four or five – all carpet colours, mustard, thyme, fondant chocolate, grey blueberry. One or two – when no one comes to let them in, they can jump out – one will be Hansel, show Gretels how it's done. These today are too many – four or five can't jump, they tumble, spring, fall back – they're like a villanelle, or propositions, contradicting, 'does not compute', are inconsistent. Like canons, repeating with different sonorities in different registers.

For them, though they are fearful and frustrated – the experience is warming. It's exercise. They hate each other, the proximity, thc limitation that prevents them stretching their wings – their arms and legs.

It fires up my philosophy! Like the guy with the tortoise on his head, or making the bath overflow.... A law of unintended consequences? Of seeking, failing, succeeding in an unforeseeable way?

They, the cats, lack intelligence – but they do much much better than we do. Do they? It's comforting to think so....

*

There was the offer.... An expedition, to Siberia, cloning woolly mammoths. Digging them out – a legion of them.

The books tell you it's where the landscape is so dull, extreme, not made at all for us – that it's other human beings who must appreciate you, you them. It is the edge, the end, roundness has finished long before you reach that frozen sea, filled with delicious various fish....

Whose idea would that have been?

But – you have to pay.

The team that clones – it's mostly cloning dogs. Pets.

I can't afford the trip

– and it's naff, the pets.

So, I miss the best experience of my life.

*

When you come back, you're wise. How do you know? It seems that the first test of wisdom would be knowing if you're wise. It doesn't turn out that way.

I don't care about the mammoths – when I've had my day, no one will clone me. Would I know? *Esprit*, mind, soul, *Geist*? Somehow something goes on, but it's collective, a Brownie snap – your mind has expired, for ever. My ghost, material ... but is it me?

Better save those who're going extinct, not resurrecting the antiquities.

Saving life: philosophers once said that it was good, they didn't say what for. Believing in creation makes you want a purpose, meaning: something must be there for something else. Sex for making kids ... and then?

Science did for most of those – extravagant – ideas.

Philosophers – they're now extinct as well.

I missed the chance of pioneering: – Inuits, Nenets, Manchus, Mongolians: meeting, and finding comradeship ... one of a team.

*

I've known Claudia all our thinking lives. We've not grown up. She wears teen clothes.

*

'White Western males – they had their gory glory day, probing the universe, making bombs to bring it down. They're going, going.... Who'll be next to climb the tree and see the view ... a panorama parched and populous...?' Claudia asks, all rhetoric.

'Because our world is one and round, and humans mostly live on land – it's attractive to think – since each one looks for wisdom and coherence in themself – the whole must follow such a rhythm, such a sound.... The future: individuals with legs?' I say. 'It isn't so.

'Most things we haven't thought about. Everything moves crabwise, or retreats, advances and retreats. It's not dialectics, it's incoherence. Better – it's interests. And motivations. Suppose – if there is no salvation in religions that offer it – there's no salvation anywhere. Without belief, there's no salvation. Otherwise, why'd you believe? And is this all, enough, for your salvation? For what, exactly?

'Marx was right and wrong, though he couldn't admit to it: – he had a politics that didn't fit into his determinism. 'What would happen, must.' If you want it different – change it, though it's impossible ... or everything is open to your will. If you've a philosophy, have it motivate you – but what will happen will happen anyway. All falls down, all is rebuilt – different, but with the same rule of contradiction – the magnificent temple must stand on the pulp of sacrificed babies ... until it falls.'

She's silenced: we look at each other, then look around the room – drab, familiar: small.

'It would have been exciting,' I say. 'Siberia. Though the aim – I'm not so sure. You get money proposing these excursions – like novel plots, movie scenarios.... Moguls give the cash, they don't even know it's gone. They only know it won't come back. It's a croupier's tip. I was keen to spin the wheel, that's all.'

To someone, I shall be a dinosaur. What was I for? I might be complete – dying young, not ravaged, having to lose pieces all along like packaging, then collapsing in old age like a dried fig.

'You're old,' says Claudia. 'But you ask the questions adolescents do. And you don't try to find the answers. You love ignorance.'

'Time back,' I say. 'We two would have been slaves.'

'Indentured,' Claudia says. 'Mine's a patrician name.'

'Workers. Proletarians,' I say. 'Now, we're nothing. Equal to the best, the richest, the most powerful, but also equal to – people like us, with nothing.'

'It's a problem dinosaurs didn't have to face,' says Claudia. 'But people aren't interested in your story. People who like stories – they don't care about us.'

'It's good,' I say. 'I don't want to entertain them. Besides, if you don't go to jail, you're conscripted. Even both.'

*

To be a person who has never known, loved, understood, hated and sympathised with another, any other: that is a tragedy. For a person never to have been understood by any other person, is a farce.

*

'The trouble with us persons,' says Claudia. 'Is we can't drop our teleology. Marx thought he'd dropped his Hegel – but there it was. And the trouble with teleology is – it has to reach its end!'

'Is that a *mot*, Claudia?' I ask, impressed. 'Remember how the Enlightened ones batted them to and fro, like before the Revolution – "*le roi n'a pas de sujets*", you might say. The king has no subjects, like after the revolution, or as a wit!'

'What do you mean?' she asks.

'It's a line in a movie. It meant that the king didn't join in these *jeux d'esprit*. Shouldn't, couldn't. Aside from his inadequacy – it would have been *lèse majesté*,' I say.

'Poor Marx,' says Claudia. 'No one knows what he really thought – he had no one to talk to. Just writing letters and meeting geniuses, and people who thought they were. You can't explain yourself by writing books.'

'What does "explaining yourself" signify?' I ask. 'Most people tell lies to get a job: explanation is not required.'

'You know that I'm in love,' she says. '*You* know, but it's impossible to tell the person I'm in love with.'

Claudia confides in me because we can't live in the world we were born into – a gritty stretch of it, place and life. With chipboard families.

She loves a merchant seaman. He's rarely docked: then for a few hours... It's better for same sex people, their hours more probably coincide. But if it doesn't catch for them, for anyone, there's nothing to be done.

*

All this was long ago. We were always adolescents together, full of knowledge, poor in wisdom.

Claudia – did she discover something? The end's the end, whether the curtain's drawn by you, or just the action finishes, there's no more lines. Did she find, and didn't want to tell? Or spied through the keyhole, saw another; vistas of keyholes without keys.

*

When Claudia died she left a note – 'What is life without wisdom? If it's missing, what is life without a compensation? The second-best of happiness, affection? All that stuff. I leave you my vase – it's full of all the good and bad things in the world – it makes no difference at all. You already have all those – and now you have my vase to keep them in.'

It's grotesque, the vase. Being grotesque – it makes no difference. Being there – that's what's important, and Claudia's mistake – is not to be anywhere at all.

*

Claudia – a loss. But – can you lose something you never had? Maybe the merchant seaman had her? – ignoble thought, but maybe others too – still more ignobility.

Death, her death – a mystery. I left it there. A mistake: her cold feet. My cold heart. There's no way further on, where death's involved – there's no mystery at all. We know it all, everything. Claudia – did she think you could take another step and find out more than you already knew?

*

Try mathematics – the formal proof is easy – she was there, now she's not. But incompleteness says that truth and meaning enter into mathematics, hover there, as an uncertainty. No truth unsullied, nothing abstract – except the maths. Coffin, hole, tears, forgetfulness, regret. But truth and meaning, where are they? – those are sore fingers. If they signify something for mathematics, which is 'here' and ascertainable, what do they signify for us: for me, for Claudia? Death – does it cancel out the meaning, or if it's part of it – what does it *mean?*

*

I volunteer for expeditions. The mammoths have been exhumed, stretched out on the slabs – but there's deserts full of stuff.

The physical side's oppressive. I'm a weedy sort, with erupting skin and peppery bowels. The reward is finding what one's looking for, attested on the list. One day, the list will be completed – ticks all over. Ticks everywhere – in my hair, my clothes, my sleeping bag.

It's all culture, mostly digging and bagging. The indigenes? ... that's quite a joke. There's never anyone around – where'd they come from anyway?

It's physical graft, harder than hammering on drums or crating old masters and mistresses, so shades don't seem to matter, shades of forgotten people, shades of truth or meaning. Skeletons of animals, of princes and prisoners, of cats and cockatoos.

*

'This was all Fatimid land,' says Khalil. 'What do you expect to find?'

The courtyards, peach and almond – the breezes ... scents of different leathers, dye-pits, soldered metals.... A shed with cassowaries....

'Excavations, I hope,' I say. 'The terra cotta degrades, you still see the shapes left in the clay. Just dig more holes.'

'Don't dig near the jail,' he says. 'You'll find what you don't want.'

'I come from people mute and indifferent,' I say. 'They know they've had their day, but don't remember when that was. We came as colonists – now, we exhume.'

'I know,' he says. 'You're a boil, we'll never be rid of you. You were our romantics, now you're here as scientists. The world's supposed to be one, but still you're here, in a clump, waving your old flag.... Your class.... My countryman, from countries I don't know.'

*

Khalil's a youth – he loves doing what he wants, and sharing it. He insists. He's a fanatic about himself.

*

'The singer,' I say. 'I want her, want her voice ... to wear it....'

'We all do,' says Khalil. 'And what's more – we all can take it, wind it round us, like silk, like a snake – it hugs us, so we become silk, snake. We become what we want, have always wanted – the missing part of us....'

'So,' I say. 'What we were before – it would be gone?'

'Yes,' he says. 'Good riddance.... Her voice, the shape of everyone you've ever coveted – is every voice, amalgamated into essence, fragrance, unguent ... it doesn't call to you, doesn't need you to be inspired ... it has no spirit ... it is substance. You are not.'

'I didn't know there were such clubs,' I say. 'Like this. With alcohol and hash....'

'No, absolutely there are not,' he says. 'You're here, enjoying it, because you're not obedient. Being disobedient, you find what you ought not. Or else – you're foolhardy. You think no one is watching. Or maybe you've cut away your conscience....'

'Yes,' I say. 'That's quite right. When I was young, I could discuss the deepest themes – where we come from, where we go, death, life, and rights – all that.... And mathematics, currents, ice palaces, why things break when dropped, and why things melt and change into a dragonfly, and eggs and chrysalides, plants, madness.... In the end, I knew about the universe, and found – I had no conscience. None at all. And moreover there was no source for one: no measure, and no use....'

'And no divinity who cared if you drank alcohol....' says Khalil. 'That was my conclusion too, arrived at by a different path....'

We smoke our pipes, and drink. Khalil offers me a friendship, information I'd not guessed at....

'You're pissed,' he says. 'Absolutely. Don't trust me. That's what you do if you're an Orientalist. That's what I am – and what you must not be.'

The singer – Fatimata – her voice follows us, supports us; then we turn a corner and it stops. I weep –

'No,' says Khalil. 'Tomorrow it can be the same. It's what maintains me – I fear no jail, no death, no void....'

'I know,' I say. 'I don't believe you, not a word, but – there is the song. That cannot be disbelieved. I know I'd find it in the club another time ... except, I'm not sure where that was....'

*

We researchers sleep badly, in small tents. I take my clothes off in the dark, and put them in my tent. I sleep, and there's my punishment – the alcohol storms up my throat and out my mouth, I can't shout out, it traps my arms and legs.... Sleep.

Astrid – her job's to negotiate our passes with the cops – unwraps me from my dream. 'Here's your clothes,' she says, tossing them in to me. 'You left them in my tent.'

'And did I sleep with you?' I ask. 'I'd dreamt....'

'Dreams and mistakes,' she says. 'Are best kept to yourself. Mind out! – in case you catch the Orientalism that is rife, infectious and incurable....'

*

The tribunal's in the open, tents are too small. But there's open – and there's open. Justice in theory doesn't take up much room. I don't believe in justice – besides, I'm guilty: and usually unjust.

Astrid says, 'It's too bad to be sent home, but....'

'Find me a home,' I say. 'And send me there.'

Astrid's not the boss – so, they let her talk, make the mistake.... She's stringy, a fine digger, brown as a hank of twine.

'We believe that excavating the past,' she says, 'provides a means of seeing how we have moved in present times ... it's an evolutionary exercise ... not based on how they built and died, but how they lived, cohabited ... and then it's us. How do we measure up ... How far we've come....'

'I thought it was just curiosity,' I say. 'I didn't know morality came in....'

'You're disobedient,' she says. 'Lax. A hedonist....'

'Coming here has given me an insight,' I tell them. 'It is – I didn't suffer from a lack of truth – just incompleteness.'

'Well,' she says, 'we're keen on truth, although the record's always incomplete. To fill it out – we must invent, impute. It's ethical imperialism, but ... we cannot say our ancestors were savages and ignorant....'

'That's what I am,' I interrupt.

'I'm glad you said it for me,' Astrid says. 'And we can't trust you to sieve the tiny things.'

*

I should have gone with mammoths. They're for cash, and the digging never ends ... cloning the warriors, raising zombie armies, generals betrayed and seers – now allowed their space and influence. And who would notice them? Would see that they were resurrected copies of the dead, now, our living saviours? Our nemeses, our avenging ancestors, great-grannies – done wrong to, and much worse....

*

Astrid says to the chief, Pierrick, 'It's nothing personal – but Raul here has read about the smallest, and the largest, things: the void that's full, the line that has no end, the end preceding what we know is only a beginning.... And now, the crash. He concludes in commonplace....'

'You should close your tent at night, Astrid,' Pierrick says. 'But you're right – what does Raul bring to us? "*Der Himmel ist dein Hut*", "Heaven is your hat." That's no use to us. We are "show and tell", not frolic and surmise....'

'He sought wisdom,' says Astrid, with regret. 'Found it, lost it. How sad!'

*

I tell Khalil – I've lost my work, their confidence. 'Science!' he says, 'I don't think that's something you can lose.'

'I wouldn't bet,' I say. 'There's many challengers. Science ... doesn't make you happy, doesn't even tell you what is happiness. No one bothers now with evidence: the universe is tricks, a box of toys and travellers tales – so, people want to live in villages and brew their hooch.'

'We're going to join the army,' Khalil says. 'They asked us anyway. We'll learn to shoot, and then desert. Maybe take a little boat somewhere. It's important that you learn to kill – there's guys all over learning to kill you.'

'I guess.' Not much convinced, I say, 'What happens when you all desert?'

'We go to jail when caught,' he says. 'If we get out, we have to do our service, doubled up.'

'It's best to desert before,' I say.

'Yes, Raul, that's genius,' he says. He's not enthusiastic. 'See, there's Lamya.' He points to a youngish, animated girl, with well-turned arms. 'You could have sex with her.'

'Oh,' I say, 'I'm only interested in relationships, not sex so much....'

'She'll give you hell,' says Khalil. 'She's not the faithful or the honest type. Why not have sex, forget the rest? Besides, you're an easy-going type – not honest, and not faithful, nothing special, no assets or accomplishments... haven't even started out ... don't hustle to impress, it won't go over, won't attach....'

'It's all quite different here,' I say. 'I thought you'd be uptight and hostile ... suspicious of me, and of each other.'

'Well,' he says. 'It's not as if we liked each other.... No one says we're tolerant.... We want what you foreign guys have got, but not with your corruption. It's a tough call, Raul.'

'I guess that thinking you're ingenuous, it's Orientalism, Khalil,' I say.

'No, it's plain naive,' he says.

'My expedition: maybe they'll give me a ticket home,' I say.

'Where might that be, your home?' asks Khalil, laughing.

*

It takes a while to locate myself in this world. Then, I remember. Of course – Futurism! That's what I'm in. Key points: 'Pure sound' and 'parts of bodies' – the singing – is it pure? Pure sound's itself an oxymoron.... Lamya is 'parts of bodies', non-metaphorical. Obsessing me. But then, I too am 'parts of bodies'. Everybody is.

'Khalil,' I say. 'One way of exiting this poetry – is finding and riding on a metaphor ... seeing the whole ambience reel back to something earlier ... Or later.

'It's like your conscription puzzle.... Obey the law, desert and go to jail. Join the other side, their army – you are bound for ever.'

*

We take a boat, Lamya, Khalil and me. To save Khalil from military service: new life in the old world? We're powerless....

'Nonsense,' says Khalil. 'Fatimata's voice will be our motor, much stronger, more reliable than those outboard things – she'll stand upon the shore....'

'Wait!' says Lamya, lifting her head from my elbow. 'Where do we go?'

'You're right,' I say. 'This is a voyage, so we need to know where it ends ... and the sea – this one at least – it has no end.'

'Mostly they end in rivers,' says Khalil. 'That won't suit us. And not all rivers end in seas.'

'Until we sort this out,' I say. 'We drift.'

*

We don't drift, we spin. Why am I here in any case? I have a different document – I can leave any time I want. The voice – Fatimata sings her canons, and her trills – our little boat goes round and round....

'Let's think again,' Lamya says. 'I'm untrustworthy – I took cash.... If we go out in open seas, the guards will take us. I took money to betray us all....'

'Then why'd you come, Lamya?' Khalil asks.

'Oh,' she says. 'Beneath the greed my heart is gold. Besides – I want to get away as much as you.'

*

Astrid says, 'Too bad, it had to end like that – you, I – the scene, the team. If you had skills, experience, you could have gone around the world, we'd find you cash ... But then, you were precipitate.'

'Being speedy's not quite like being unwise,' I say. 'Maybe things weren't right, and maybe another direction opened up....'

'It's true,' she says, 'that things are almost never right. And as you tumble down the rock – an infinity of other endings flashes out. You'd have found that digging out our past makes comradeship – like actors on a movie set, a spell that holds us, disciples, Sufis ... But – when you don't know what to do, you keep on doing what you do.'

'Khalil,' I say, 'he shows you round. Perhaps – you'd get his soldiering postponed ... talk to them, Astrid ... they've got so many guys to train to shoot ... so many then desert, or join the other side ... the underground ... one less....'

'Be prudent, Raul,' she says. 'You know it's history, all that. No one will stop it just for you, because you are infatuated....'

'It's species-being, Astrid, agate-cool – not love or friendship, not those flowery shades....' I say.

*

'Is Fatimata on tonight?' I ask Khalil.

'It's new,' he says, quite sad. 'A modern group, crossing over and quite loud.'

'Here, Raul,' Lamya says. 'You ought to kiss me more. I'm running risks for you....'

Close up, she's older, much, than what you thought. Her mouth tastes medicated, like stuff for a sore throat, to hide another taste.... Her upper lip – is stiff, like a plaster carnival mask....

The group is very loud. There's a bigger, younger, more enthusiastic public. You can hear them outside, in the street – not so much transgression as affront.

*

Khalil disappears. Lamya, alas, does not – she clings. It's not her fault: no blame, but still....

'Men prefer to join the other side,' says Astrid. 'So's to avoid the army – the army of the state. They think they can desert quite easily ... or find a group that shares their views.... It isn't so. Most don't come back. And if they do.... They wish they'd stayed away.'

'Khalil says, if there's intelligent life out there, in the blue that's really black ... that can talk to us – it must see us as a dog, or sheep. Routinised, incontinent, take us for walks, or eat us....' I say.

'We all think that and wonder, Raul,' says Astrid. 'Forget about intelligence. You'll get the blame for Khalil running. We'll need bundle you up and ship you out, or things will be bad here – mostly for you, but us as well. Is there anyone you'd like to tell?'

'Oh, absolutely not,' I say. 'Let this big adventure end with a little one ... anonymous....'

'We'll crate you up,' she says. 'And load you on a cargo: a cutty-pipe, you'll look like Conrad, and we'll read your stories....'

I think she means to joke.

'Khalil's in error,' she goes on. 'Those camps – they're asking to be rocketed. Of course – we're a camp, a target too, but someone will avenge us.'

'I need an expedition,' I say. 'With those, you know what there is to find, but you don't know how or when – it's ideal for people like me – curious, but needing stability. Just wandering is out.'

'Forget it, Raul,' says Astrid sharply. 'It's colonialism – call it cultural, if you like. More world empire, appropriating, delving down, culling the abundant, nurturing the few.... Ecology instead of phrenology, zoo harvesting instead of slaves, slaves instead of massacres.... If we load Lamya on, will you take over her two kids?'

'If you're right, Astrid, there's no way out. Philosophy is obsoleted so that science can take over whoever's not informed and primed....' I say. I'm shaken, though.

'That leaves rocketing, and bathyscapes. You want palaces or furry animals – it's juvenile, I fear,' she says. 'But bathyscapes – it's fish, of course, and cold, greenish dark. The rockets – you need an excellent aim – it's mostly soldiers up there, in the pods – but look at the contracts – ninety-six years, three hundred ... that won't do for you....'

'You've sympathy, Astrid,' I say. 'Maybe you're all-round *sympathique.*'

'Oh,' she says. 'I'm not the understanding type.You mean Khalil? He's an insurgent. Watch out – they're terrorists. I categorise, I don't encourage or enthuse.'

'I admit,' I say. 'I'm not a student of people. I never studied. I could do better if I tried, I'm sure, but better? For what? Better than what? It may be "better than history" – everybody says you must understand it, the influence it has – but it's invisible, an interpretation, experience we never had, that maybe no one did, lies and hearsay, rhodomontade and secrets, cover-ups and cover stories.... Even if you know – there is no wisdom, and no truth.

'And, Astrid – archaeology; what you're supposed to do – they say it's fundamental, even glamorous – but it's the stupid grandfather, illiterate, his brain is porridge, winnowed, drained down his nose by reeds.... They say – "once you had the bible, we had the land, now – we have the bible, and you have our land...." The poor land is here, chickens farmed for Antwerp, packed corpses all night and day in throbbing factories....'

'How you skitter, Raul,' Astrid says, and laughs. 'You'll never lead the struggle!'

'I'm not a missionary,' I say. 'I'm an apostate.... These guys want Lebensraum, I fold in small, I have no interests....'

'That's where you're wrong,' she says. 'Our music, Raul! We could have made some, but you're an absolutist.... The world's not made of solutions, it's made of icebergs drifting by. Hop on, hop off. Claudia – she followed you, longing for a path that led somewhere. And then she saw – your desert's trackless.... On, on, you have to go, the wind blows and your tracks – they disappear.... She dies, a rare fruit in the sand, that dessicates and fossilises.... Uneaten. Inedible.'

*

Lamya says, 'You need not have worried – no one stays with anyone for long, not now. I'd have taken a short trip with you – you wanted eternity, dumped me – and so I have no choice. I must betray you, keep my honour, and myself in play....'

*

'This local woman....' Pierrick says. 'There is a complication. Raul broke his word to her, it seems. And there's the cops – they say Raul's in touch with terrorists.... It's not as if he cared for what we do – our project. Slack Jack, I'd call him....'

I'm here. In front of him.

'No, that isn't so,' I say. 'I dug deep – maybe not always in the end where you said, but in the wherefore of what the expedition meant....'

'And reached no conclusion,' Pierrick says. 'Astrid had to tell you most about it.'

'That is the way,' I say. 'We climb up other people's backs, their wisdom becomes our footnotes....'

He doesn't need to seem convinced.

They cut me off. It's good, I'm on my own – it's bad too – here, you need someone to cover you.

*

I'm a savage. It's good. I can't read the writing, don't understand the language – a joke, an insult, or a question, it's all the same to me: a stake in the eye? *That* speaks to me, but no one dares. I'm dirty. No one wants. I slink and cower. I crouch, I trot, I frighten donkeys.... Where am I going? Anywhere? Or do I become the furniture – and will they feed me, leave worn-out stuff that I can wear – and will they think I'm human? Eat their food? Put on their clothes? Resist the evil eye, and make the signs?

A frontier, something well-defined, a river, marsh or wilderness – requires negotiation. Those guys over there, like me but speaking differently, dressed, odd, and dirty, hair knotted up.... I'd not feel safe with them....

*

I'm sure that's how it went, so long ago. Begging. Smaller animals, hunted, trapped – fair game, that is the phrase.

Begging, eating dead meat, totting stuff ... fruit hanging overhead.... That's the normal – progress, evolution, the normality. Or I could think big and start a bank, 'beg big' – my slogan! Or run a book.

Claudia – she might have been a sister, unacknowledged, and there'd be no impediment, no incest barrier, though she was muscular, larger than me, and stronger too, I'd bet.... Died young, but if she'd been a savage, she'd have lived right through, what everyone expects, an average time.... Enough to find out everything.

*

What joy! Here's a frontier, a border. You cross it – but you're not yet there, not in the other place, but you are on the way.... I can read everything. The language – becomes comprehensible. I see the difference between a joke, an insult.

There's an official – maybe she is here to assist, to make a conversation, make you feel at home, although you're not, and she has her home, not yours to give or take.

'Are you Aziza?' I ask. 'Or is that the badge you all wear on this shift?'

'You make no sense,' she says. 'We're all diffferent. Forget the badge. I am Aziza – forget the other one, the other Azizas....'

'That should be easy. I have experience in forgetting,' I say. We laugh.

'You must be pleased to get away,' she says. 'You were a savage, now you're civilised. And were the others savages?'

'No, no,' I say. 'It's not complex. They were right in everything they do, and they are right when saying what they do is wrong.'

'We're much the same as where you were,' she says. 'But different. What we do is right for us....'

This could go on for ever, this rambling round: 'Enough!' I say. 'It's enough I understand and talk to you....'

'You're naive, Raul,' she says. 'It's not at all enough. I have a pistol by my side. That doesn't talk at all.'

'You're here to make me feel at home, Aziza....' I say, hoping....

'I have a home,' she says. 'I'll take you there, it is my job, but it will never be your home. And you won't stay: don't get excited. People come and go – it is the right arrangement – just don't hang around. Come in, and then be ready to be booted out.'

'You're easy to understand, Aziza,' I tell her. 'But hard to comprehend.'

'It's so all over, Raul,' she says. 'We oscillate between clinging to our nature and accommodating all the rest....'

'The rest – that must be history, I guess,' I say. 'What isn't nature ... is experience.' The subject drops.

'Look at my boots!' she says. 'You'll find them sexy – they'll cause a pang, when the time comes to boot you out....'

'I guess....' I say: they're tall and shiny. Sexy? Hmmmm.

She lounges – her white glitter pants light up the black leather divan. We cluster round on pouffes and ottomans.

'You'll work, Raul,' she says. 'For me, and cash. I'm in the moral sphere. I work for free. Everything in me's about morality.... No dead meat served, my love....'

'Just sugar mice and gingerbread,' I say. We laugh.

'I am a volunteer,' she says. 'I have the moral ground. I've found a home for you. You're in the market-place – morality is not involved with you.'

I never see the promised work.

I leave it there.

*

Slowly, I move towards wisdom, perhaps I'll reach it before I die. It's not much prized.

Aziza runs a band, a gathering of lions or wolves, except we're all emaciated, left our paws and tails in traps. We don't go out to hunt – we sit round Aziza, and she picks our lice. I'm the last arrival, a vagabond returning, half-in, a mascot. It's a matriarchy. The big males that drop in and make the cubs – they do not stay. She's a volunteer, a moral being – she and her friends, they hunt, take in the living. It's good – it's not the best.

'Fulfil yourself, Raul,' she says. 'Eat! Don't ask questions without answers!'

She holds our strings, and jerks us into life, men, women, and the dogs.... Except – it's not our life, it's hers: 'You must get used to lady bosses, their morality – you can't pay it off, nor flatter me, my sex comes from the fashion store,' she says. 'You want tranquillity, and I want power – dance, all of you, do quadrilles, reel and twist ... I love to see you hop, and twitch along when the music's stopped....'

Aziza – she recruits – for the regime, its opposition too. These salons – for some the gilded chair, for others – the electric one. For all – time's guillotine. For some, it's real, for others, it's a metaphor, that people nowadays don't grasp. Realism has won – it's gobbled up the magic and the fantasy – realism that's like junket, sliding off, nothing you can touch or smell.... Aziza – the leading edge, our future. Everyone's. I'm not convinced – this way, you get a clique, a mafia, a giunta. They'll know who you are....

*

We're beached. We have vinyl evenings – the Amazons, the picked-up guys, me and Travi; Piotr the alpha guy, just moving through. Under the talk and quips there's Sorcerer playing, and Pierrot. They go spinning round.

*

'These people here,' Travi says, 'have made peace with their neighbours, so they can send their mercenaries all round elsewhere; make war, say they mediate: they don't lose anything. But the massacres! – they are immense. Aziza denies it all, and we're her proof, we live in idleness...! She is a benefactor, best of guys....'

'It's time to run away,' I say. 'It's inconclusive, but here, we are in amber.... We don't eat the animals, but they go on the same as ever, eating each other. There is no other way....'

'Don't expect to change it,' Travi says. 'You must reach a higher stage, and then rejoice. Cling on. Don't sign up, don't be conscripted, don't be a mercenary. If Aziza says you have to go back, over there, to make the peace – don't believe her. And don't go.'

'I know,' I say. 'To avoid doing good, I've had to sleep rough many times. I've no substance, not here nor there. Aziza drains your blood....'

'They say you should keep life simple,' Travi says. 'I don't know why they think it's good that way. We're surrounded by ambiguous types – they hold us tight, to show they're generous. It isn't so. Everyone is worried for our mental health, in case we take an axe to them.

'Live by a river, and you're clean: beside a lake – your ego languishes and stinks.'

*

Travi's very tall. I climb up him, stand on the compound wall. He's like I was – a savage, not reading, speaking, any useful tongue. I can't pull him up after me, and he can't climb. If I'm discrete, I can escape.

I say, 'Aziza wins the moral game ....'

'She plots,' says Travi. 'It's politics, I'm sure.'

She's quite inscrutable.

‘She’s your sovereign, Travi,’ I shout. ‘You must expect the tyranny.’

Travi – my best friend. I’ll leave him here. There is no choice – besides, I’ve heard his story many times: he’s shown me all his depths, and told his jokes.

I jump down in the dust. I don’t call out to Travi – anything would be a trick, a lie, even to say goodbye – they might hear, catch me, and I’d be back.

Here before me is the choice – the sandy steppe, or the low mountains, fold on fold ... like green table linen....

Both landscapes are repetitive. I choose the sand – it takes less effort, but is barren.

Here’s an old grey wooden door, lain in the yellow-beige. I lie on it, can’t sleep. Then beat out a rhythm. It heaves up. It opens, throwing me off....

‘Yes?’ asks a spry oldish man, down in his hole.

‘I’d hoped to be alone,’ I say, by way of apology.

‘You’re wise,’ he says. ‘I might have shot you through the letterbox. Or knifed you through the spyhole. Red-hot pokered you through the keyhole.... So, maybe your hoping – was not so wise.’

‘I see you’re seeking wisdom,’ he says, taking me into his house. ‘I don’t advise it. It does no good to anyone. You’re set apart, and cannot communicate. You can’t teach wisdom. People will get bored with you ... and fast.’

‘They’re bored anyway....’ I start to say, but can’t develop more – his house is enormous ... rare pictures on the walls. ‘Oh,’ he says. ‘The enormity is mirrors – they’re cleaned every so often, they multiply all space ... if you have a palace, it needs maintenance all year....’

It's so: the place is tiny, but the mirrors give it a depth, room opens on to room, it's Versailles before the executions ... and before they take the pictures down....

'Oh, I'd have to save up to get one of them original,' he says. 'And it would look lonely, all alone.... This way I have them all – repros in mags – I crumple each one when I'm tired of it.... In this album,' and he lifts down a leathery tome, 'I have copshots of the most ambitious robbers. If they want to steal the pics, I show them the mugshots.... That's what they're really interested in – the competition. Fame. I have pictures of banknotes too ... they can steal those....'

'You seem wise,' I say. 'Though other terms apply: foresightful ... illuded ... paranoid ... self-protective....'

'I'm sure those all come in,' he says. 'In my head, there are addresses, and equations too. Scenes of slaughter, reels of unmade movies ... partners had and disappointed ... horses disqualified and horses nobbled ... all locked away, safe and never on display. That is wisdom too.'

'You make it all seem banal,' I say. 'I have endured....'

'Of course you have,' he interrupts. 'Your heart still beats. I see you vertical before me. All your adventures went off half-cock, flashes in the pan, wads shot, misfires, your breeches blocked, as they say – you're all too human....'

And he laughs.

*

'Now,' he says. 'Tell me what you know – not the permanent, the moribund, not what gasps in this night-breathed air, all the life snorted out, sucked back in – but what is going on. What's happening? Who's up, who's down, who's spying, who's lying, who will win, who will survive...'

'What stuff is that?' I ask. 'Journalism? History before it happens?'

'Yes,' says the sage. 'What's going to happen. More important than wisdom, that, and no one seems to know. Or tell. I don't mean who is guessing, buying stuff in, hoarding – what's the end-game, who wins this joust...?'

He looks eagerly at me, and I see he knows, suspects – nothing. Nothing at all.

*

I tell him what's going to happen.

He's silent. Then, 'Well, of course, it's foreseeable. Poor people have always gone to the wall. But after all the promises – that it should go on in that way.... Of course, I have my pension....' And he realises.... 'And there's a girl who brings me bread and milk – and of course, she's a delight – tit bits with my tidbits, you'll have heard that many times....'

'No one cares,' I say. 'All that was yesterday....'

'Of course,' he says, 'there's the temperature. And the scarcity; and the big universal brain does all the work....'

'It's dirty work,' I say. 'What's to be done. And you're not an enthusiast – don't have the full pizzaz.... If you're too wise, you don't care enough. Then they don't pick you up when you fall down.'

'You're right,' he says, mournfully. 'I'm wise enough to recognise you're right, and I am shafted.... Of course, there must be ways of organising things so that being poor is not my sole concern. I know – there's justice and fairness, restraint and resistance too – but I'm here, on my own. People that I meet – they're like you, on *their* own or stupid. Usually both.... If not that, they're greedy.'

'Travel brings that on,' I say. 'I'm not wise, but I know a lot, much more than you, old sage. I shan't ever be wise, and I don't care – I prefer to travel round, expand myself.'

'You have many people after you,' says the sage, Lennox. 'You have to keep on running, but catching you won't do them any good – no, none at all.'

We chew on this paradox.

'Death. Desertion, desperation – terror and flight,' I say. 'I've witnessed these. And then dependency and boredom, betrayal of my friends and lovers – sometimes the agent, sometimes the sufferer....'

'Yes, yes,' says Lennox. 'Most things it is best to witness. Death, for instance. Don't try to suffer that direct.'

We laugh.

'You will survive, for sure,' he says, hugging me. 'But what'll happen in my case? If it rains – the water'll come straight in my front door ... snow through the keyhole. Science! I hope they've got it right.'

'I try to avoid what other people say,' I say.

'Yes!' says Lennox. 'Distrust experience. Distrust truth revealed or operating; people who see God or virgins, or who make telephones and saxes ... usually what they make does not exist, or is a trolley that conveys banalities, is but a vehicle, shifts its shape, has none....

'Witness! Evade! Yes! You have that right! You're far outside the precedents. Don't go on stage to prove it, though .... that way, more commonplace results. You'd be one of a troupe of clowns who weep real tears – how dull!'

'I'm glad you appreciate me, Lennox,' I say. 'But what does your appreciation mean? You're protected – I'm exposed. You've taken all the precautions anybody can. You're in a burrow – asking me in, ushering me out. So what?'

'What it is, has been. Blink – the new scene is real, what was – is history, is failed philosophy. And nothing more,' he says, shutting the door.

*

This is the savour, gravy, juice and lymph of life, I think: good counsel from a sage, who's underpowered, intimidated. I'm reassured, for no good reason. But there remains the question – sustenance. Cash, food. The old sage Lennox said there was a girl, Mahnaz, a guardian angel, who brought food and titillation. Years ago, I'd be accused of being a freeloader, and a strong-arm guy – exploiting women, exploiting old-fashioned sex, all that. Now – no one cares. I don't get anywhere with anyone.

I scout around. There's no one here. This is a desert, after all: in the mountains, it would be different, perhaps....

Mahnaz says, 'Take heart! Great movements – they have ended in the sand, but come from there as well.... Drink this camel's milk – in all your life, you'll need no other fuel – you'll trot for ever, if you drink enough....'

Mahnaz is slender as a twig: a gopher's features, and her pitch is shrill and unrelieved ... until she sees you need some truth from her, washing down the crumbs of knowledge you might have. Then, you see – she's full of power, an everlasting battery, whatever holds the stars and asteroids up in the sky: a force.

It gets dark, really dark, considering there's so much sky. A shock – you realise you're on a liner, just the one deck – perhaps there's Lennox in an engine-room, but without motors, there's no sound – 'Where do we sail at night?' I ask Mahnaz.

'Nowhere,' she says. 'It's like standing still. They decided that a century ago – space is full. For us, it's time, but there's no time here, it stopped when the trees and grass died and went to be our curse – the gasoline beneath.

'If only, Raul – we had transport, a put-put, a moto ... see, the town ahead....'

It's lighted like a pin-cushion, bright tiny heads – 'I'm a guide,' says Mahnaz. 'I tell lies. It is expected. I'm an outcast.'

'I'm too ambitious to check up on you,' I say. 'Lies, truth – it's all the same, I don't check, I don't believe a word....'

'That's what Lennox says,' she says. 'But if you do without words, you don't get very far.'

'It sounds like Quine,' I say, but Mahnaz doesn't laugh, maybe she doesn't hear.

There's people standing round. 'All these kids are ready for you,' Mahnaz says. 'They'd be your arms and legs. Organise them. They will organise you – you'll lead us where we want to be....'

'I'm not like that,' I start. 'I'm not a leader.'

'No, you should be,' Mahnaz says. 'Be generous, an optimist. I can't stand you old guys – you smell like falling trees, full of parasites and nests, all moribund.'

'What will happen to Lennox?' I ask.

'Nothing,' she says. 'Here, have a bigné. That will do us for the next days, until we have transport. And a plan. Lennox will stay in his lair. Whatever he told you, between you and me, Raul, there is no sexual trade. You're old enough to understand – Lennox is much older. He didn't understand.'

'All these lives, Mahnaz, spent standing round, in anger,' I begin... I'd have preferred something pistacchio. I eat the bigné nonetheless. 'They are petards, smouldering....'

She finds me a room. 'I have no cash, Mahnaz,' I say.

'If you're a big soul,' she says. 'It's of no consequence. If not – sneak out – don't wait around for me – the end, goodbye!'

Who ever thought of charging someone for their sleep?

*

How I miss the forest – the spookiness, the hierarchy, everyone in squads, to each its food, its prey, its order – the rich times and the long winters ... sleep. Or prowl, go beyond what you should consume, leave the pack, desert your progeny ... run and howl, kill the sleepers, kill the solitaries....

I miss the bigné – Mahnaz says to go without; hunger toughens you, and sharpens too.

‘Write and read,’ she says. ‘But don’t go out. I’ll bring you what I can....’

It isn’t much, it’s not enough. ‘You are not here for fun,’ she says. ‘You are a blade, a point, all that matters is how sharp.’

‘Whatever I am here for, it’s not what I can do, what I might do,’ I say.

‘You only need to be a mystery,’ she says. ‘The rest will be the history.’

I’m in prison here, my room ... Mahnaz my jailer, my silent comrade. My structure. I was made for this, my solitude, and now it starts to fester....

It’s all lived life, until it’s not.

I don’t believe that. Life, my life, has not begun. A surprise to come.

If this is prison, where’s the animal I make as a pet? The prisoner in the next room, decapitated at dawn? Where’s the lesson, the proof?... I’m a former president, my family died on a Tuesday, poisoned, every one of them, by marrons glacés.... I discovered the truth, hid it from my jailer, forgot it when they told me I would be released. The floor and walls are made of branches – orange monkeys and brown foxes hunt the sausage fruit that grows each morning.

None of that. None of that, nothing, is true. Not even the hallucinations. I vomit the bad food, all day I lie in foetal panic knowing I shall not be born. When the door opens, I am dead, I disappear.

‘Let me go,’ I tell Mahnaz. ‘I know nothing, have done nothing. I realise – it is a game. An insult to the innocents – I’m a wastrel, a trimmer, betrayer of no cause....’

'I expected this,' she says. 'You're not a friend of people here – they're idlers, hedonists and pacifists. They grumble – you're not here for that, you're kept here to be rigorous, correct. You are a missionary, Raul ...It's your big, last, chance – a father to the people, people who aren't yours, father when the fathers are derided, all their day is done. But nonetheless....'

'It isn't what I want,' I say. 'You may think I am a mahdi, that you've made – a general, a sacrifice, a beacon, soldier; expendable, insignificant. A martyr? Warrior? A sleeper.... Yet – I've no nostalgia, no regret for anything that was, was wanted. If you bring arms, a retinue – more shackles! I'm the sleeper who does not wake....'

'Yes,' she says, 'you are a model prisoner – a sleeping one.' She laughs, she finds in me a depth of funniness.... I'm a raven in a cage, if I could walk, I'd waddle, if my wings were whole – I'm too heavy to flutter up and out, through the hole between the wall and roof.

I was to be the foreigner, deliverer, the untainted. I am not. No one is – and still I failed....

On Friday, there's a demo – all the young men, and many young women demonstrate – they want work, they want the political system that might begin to guarantee them – then a useful life. These are subjects I never had the time to raise with Lennox, or with any of my other contacts. Mahnaz says, 'You're incorrigible. You're totally passive. My plan was to present you as a foreigner, a powerful, mysterious figure, come to mobilise.... No one was interested in you as a subject.

'.... early days, of course. You were in danger, but here, in your cell.... I was more threatened – but you ... you were yourself! Even the madeleine, your godforsaken bigné. Your idea of sacrifice and personhood. I could have done better, if I had been you. It's a myth, your being just yourself, hoping it will all work out.... You must see – there's no point in anyone staying here, silent all day in the heat and then talking loud till late – you'll surely have heard it all.'

'It was ridiculous, Mahnaz,' I say. 'Your plan ... it's brought out exactly how I'm not suitable.'

'I've found someone who appreciates me,' she says. 'Armin.'

'Good for you,' I say. 'I nearly starved there, and I must owe for my cell. I was your prisoner – now I must thank you for releasing me, because I'm no longer profitable....'

'At least you know you're wise, Raul,' she says. 'Though it's done neither of us much good.'

'You found your Armin,' I say. 'I was rash to seek you out and go along with you, your plan. Although – it's life.'

'Knowing about you,' she says. 'Doesn't mean anybody knows about me. Do I want them to? If it changes everything ... do I want that?'

'You placed your bets on Armin,' I say. 'He could be plausible: trust your judgement, trust other people. Live on the high-wire. I hear you quiz me: 'wisdom' – that's my prey. Is it more than caution, scepticism regarding everything? Any idiot can distrust and misbelieve whatever they are told. If that is wisdom, it is also ignorance. A copout, self-rejection – you disbelieve what you are told, you're sceptical about what you see, what you experience. Nothing is left for you, you flounder in a shallow pool.... I understand, Mahnaz. You have to soldier on....'

'That's it exactly,' she says. 'That's the point. Being free: – the soldier has a gun – but is she free? If you've money, you can be free: if you've none at all – that too. But mostly, just a little. It's what we all have, like a little fever, a little death inside. Do we want it, anyway, to be free? Doing something of what we want – is that what we mean? To do with wanting, desire; not freedom, not at all.'

'You mean sex?' I ask. 'Love?'

'Love, even sex – they make you feel good in yourself. Love, sometimes. Sex – briefly, not often. Is it worth a life spent chasing that?' she asks.

'I can't answer you, Mahnaz,' I say. 'You ask because you know I cannot answer. Everyone's expected to, to have an answer. I go along with what you say – there are machines where two cogged racks, set with teeth, use each other to climb up the other, to escape.'

'We need a cart like that, to take us out the desert,' says Mahnaz. 'The Americans – they're keen to have us live like them, they say, so in a day or so we'll maybe reach a city, built and working just like theirs, their rules, working their way, saluting flags, and carrying a gun....'

'And where do we fit in?' I ask.

'A box, stupid,' she says and laughs. 'In a box. What fits in a box? Anything at all, unless it is a larger box.'

*

Armin? She never mentions him again.

Here, there are soldiers, some in big trucks, trundling along like elephants in file, others in little jeeps like grasshoppers.

'You must take a side, Raul,' says Mahnaz. 'But don't trust either, nor me, nor yourself. The soldiers helped destroy this town. It wasn't going anywhere; now – it won't survive. What can you offer us, Raul?'

'I went on expeditions for the fun, because it was out of time, out of the present. Only the present has time,' I say. 'The past has none, the future isn't there – or maybe it is scattered as a present, innumerable, in bedrooms and burrows, clouds that think and spit.

'The future's waiting for us somewhere. Time in the present – a tick, a tock, it's gone. Down the pipe. I don't think about it.... History – not of much use: it's a perspective.... peering into shadows, seeking out the ghosts ... a lullaby, or a scaring tale.... You look for shapes, old friends and new in history – in the end, it's only you. Or someone you don't know, don't want ... who comes by night, sits on your bed, sticks a long beak in your flesh....'

'Well,' she says, 'without time, nothing exists on the earth – and even so, it's drift and dross, always degenerating.... How can we explain where we have come to, and if there's anywhere that we can go?'

'I'll entertain you, Mahnaz,' I say. 'Unravel the ideas, see if they convince....'

*

The world? Humans work, they want to survive, to procreate, build termite cities. Abstraction's quite another thing. The people don't fit that at all.

Work: it's almost all irrelevant, it's cleaning out the nest, or wasting time – but – there you are, stuck on this revolving clinker, burning up around its fire.... And capital, indifferent to you, a silken sack, an atmosphere you cannot breathe, that settles like a dragon's breath, moves on, leaves you incinerated, your daughters raped, sequestered.... Your avenging sword rusty and blunt....

It's for ever, the now with its fairy-tale of history ... and we are always slaves. Or else we make the world explode; all dies – so we're not here. Our role, our hope of action, disappears. Nothing happens except process. It goes on, for ever – we sally to and fro....

*

'In the end, we become the object of an expedition – inspired by curiosity,' Mahnaz says. 'Us, looking. You, looking for us because we are exotic ... at war ... traditionals ... unemancipated. You – are Others: scanning us, as we move about in herds and flocks. We're counted, and discounted. That's what you think, Raul. You discovered me – you didn't need to dig. We're all known quantities, the risks are calculated. You think we think in other sequences, in other codes.'

'I'll put it in another way. God was benevolent,' I say. 'Once, we were unisex. The seasons changed for beauty's sake – the colours changed, a metamorphosis. Then, He got pissed off. We used the seasons for festivities – to dance and drink, and cock a snook.... He threw the whole scheme down – flung dust all over, made a universe, full of wise people unable to communicate, vast distances apart. He invented death ... and aging, that made us wither, like dried figs; made sexes; divisions meangingless and indiscriminate....'

She laughs.

'Of course,' I say. 'That's all a metaphor. I just made everything up, I improvised.'

'You don't do well, Raul,' she says. 'There's states, there's politics....'

'Power comes in,' I say. 'It's how what is produced is managed and appropriated. Power: and class....'

'So – the abstraction ... the cloud you're always looking up for....' she says. 'Blocking the light...?'

'Power. Class,' I say. 'Those are abstractions. Concrete abstractions, but all the same....'

'Meantime,' she says. 'You can do anything, Raul, despite your awful start.... Just leave....'

'Your start, Mahnaz,' I say. 'Disastrous too. You have to find your course too. We – we're all high priests, or prophets. The high priests bake the prophets in clay shrouds. The prophets pull the temples down....'

'And the rest?'

'Oh,' I say. 'I left some people out? They must be the photographers, loitering round. They can't be slaves, they've been abolished ... maybe there's nothing left for them to do...? Those excavations, Mahnaz, that so attract – are they graves or the foundations of a golden house? And you – on the edges of the hole. Have you decided? What next?'

'Not yet,' she says. 'It's true, I teeter.'

'Tales,' I say, 'all tales. All useless, truth trying, having, to bury itself as fiction – we, the rich family – a goat on the breakfast table, milked directly on our oats. We, the poor, drink a cocktail of kerosene, jump off the crane for dares – here we are, trodden, busted beetles, all crawling in iron cages, our broken legs welded by the benefactor ... on feast days, gnawing neighbours' bones – and then: the drama! The camp, the prison, running, falling ... a sister redeemed, the brothers torn in strips ... and all the truth laid out, Mahnaz, and then forgotten, trivial. It has to become a fiction so we can remember it, then we forget. That's what it has to be.'

'You mustn't trust me, Raul,' she says.

'You put me in a box, a bare room, door locked, no light or air,' I say. 'You have a plan. So, I clearly couldn't trust you.'

*

'We're in a forest, Raul,' Mahnaz says. 'The trees! Talk among themselves, but not to us. The animals – they're savage, unforgiving, hungry. It's wild and uncommunicating – but somehow we must live there, conserve, and nurture....

'We live poor – and we want power. The people: those who reason like us, how far will they go, how big a change? If we save the world, all suffer, some survive, not all of them, but they'll live poor. Very poor. Lots of them, if we don't exploit the earth, they'll live quite bad, for ever. Everything will change, change permanently. Will humans manage, on their own?'

'Maybe it won't take managing, Mahnaz,' I say. 'People will wander where they can. It's good. It isn't bad.'

'Your problem, Raul,' she says, 'is shapes. Order. On every relationship you project a form it ought to fit. You pester people to make a nest the way you want. It never is. People just leave.... There's why your unhappiness....'

'Relationships?' I ask. 'Not high up on my list of troubles. Rather – you starved me, Mahnaz – but it's you that's thin. There's a fable there, somewhere....'

'It must be my heroin,' she says. 'With luck, it's always in the cities here – there's enough to keep you functioning but not so much you just fall down....'

'About the thinness,' I tell her. 'It's legend. The empty warning on the box. Don't give it heed.'

'I need the time,' she says. 'The clock – it moves too fast – repetitive, confined....'

'What you are going to do,' I say. 'You have to do yourself, Mahnaz.'

'Ah yes,' she says. 'The things I cannot do. Song and dance.'

'I was wrong about you,' I say. 'I thought you were a spirit – of the desert, the oasis.... Instead, you're someone who knows everything, and isn't nice about it. That's knowing, not being wise. You took from Lennox while you fed him....'

'I took everything from him, the very little that he had,' she says. 'But left him spry, to live and give. But don't imagine there's enlightenment, or a cloth in me that you can cut and wear. The people I have known were scum, and I don't have a style to make them live, be interesting. They're not going to memorialise and exaggerate so that I'd have to dialogue and set the record straight.... With me – silence. You thought me young – not so! I'm very very old, that's why I'll die young....'

'I confess,' I say, 'I'm not a judge of people.'

'If you were,' she says, 'you'd start off with yourself.'

'The whole of thought – my thought,' I say, 'is based on that, you're the human quality; uncertainty.'

'Oh Raul,' she laughs, 'I'm sour and disappointed, weak of will and sentiment. However hard I tried – I'd let you down, and hand you in, betray you, sell you if you had a price, deride you, forget your last defining words, and maybe pour our water store into the sand to spite – you, and me too....

'I'm that kind of girl, Raul....' And she flaps her arms, like a vindictive crow....

*

'You like expeditions, Raul, like the sound of them,' she says. 'Suppose I devise one for you....'

'You'd find a way to rob me, Mahnaz,' I say.

'What's your life worth, Raul?' she asks. 'And your rights? Of course I'd steal from you – you're worth nothing. I might make a buck from you, your innocence, your gullibility. You're a symbol, what are symbols worth? There's lots around. What do you seek? Animals? You protect them – another lot of beasts will eat as many as they can.... Religions? Antiques? There's many still to be dug up – no one knows about them, so they've not been missed. No one collects now ... except to invest. I'll invest in you, Raul.

Don't let Khalil and his guys hold you to ransom – there's no pay off here.... Not a fanam, Raul.'

'Yes, Mahnaz,' I say. 'Punish! Indulge me! What else is there?'

'A coronation? Crowned Tsar?' she asks. 'Can't you hear – *Slava! Slava!* All standing round, waiting for handouts – and you the pure, the lamb, dolled up to be the sacrifice, the strutting money-box....'

'Yes, Mahnaz,' I say. 'That appeals. How it appeals!'

'Claim some land!' she says. 'Free slaves! Feed your people. Enjoy the feeling – not many can – it beats making a movie, fucking a model....'

'I can't disagree,' I say, carried away.... 'Science, religion, common sense – whatever mode of thought you're jogging in – who'd not assent?'

'Your problem is,' she says. 'Work. We all face it. If you work hard, it's exhausting and you don't get anywhere. If you slack – you're nowhere from the start. No, it's the top job, or something quite unique – own your field, and plant it with your seeds. Whatever comes up – eat it – no one else is worthy, maybe they don't recognise what it is....'

'What's in all this for you?' I ask, still full of blood and joy: and the vision, even if it shimmers....

'Oh,' she says. 'I'm Bosch's owl. I watch. And maybe you don't recognise – this is hell. It seems the everyday to you.'

'That's so,' I say, still transformed with ambition, fulfilment, the distance.... 'Of course, the owl presides. Wisdom – I'd almost forgotten: that's my theme.'

She doesn't respond. I doubt that wisdom's what she's looking for. Assistant to a wise man – she's been that, it didn't fruit. Anyway, that fruit comes sour as quinces.

It's fantasy ... neither of us wants to engage: not with anyone, their problem ... a species fractured beyond repair, seeking, led, leading, to disaster ... when conflicts seem resolved – when societies coalesce, the result is terrifying. Mostly – they don't, and all is inconclusive – the populations move, like herds of buffalo roaming for a fresh spot with food and water.

'If you don't want, can't get, power ... and aren't a guru – what use are you to me?' she asks. 'And it's reciprocal. You're a lunatic, Raul – I love them, love them all, the lunatics. I envy them. But....'

'But maybe I should look for work – asbestos mines, or stoning plums?' I ask.

'The choice,' she says. 'There's work. It's all to make people well and safe, secure and rescued. Selling arms, pitching tents, curing the glanders, putting out fires and starting them – it's all the same, and you get paid.

'There's love – mostly, that costs, it isn't paid: – and you can't do it, Raul, nor can I. The rest is gambling. Keeping a book – letting the punters cheat their luck? Of course, for those who organise the book – it's only work. Maybe – that roundabout, the roll of dice, is what you started with: the expedition. It's what you don't know: a where or what.... You find it's gone, was never there; was hidden another spadeful deep. You frightened it away? A bug – you crushed it in your sleep?'

'You left out power,' I say. 'That has bits of all the rest. People are scattered everywhere, but power can make them sing, or dance.... Millions.'

*

'There's a message,' Mahnaz says, 'from the police. You have to report, go to them....'

'I knew it!' I say. 'Which side are you on, Mahnaz? Theirs? Or mine? It's not for deportation this time – they want to keep you. You're their humble pie, they'll spread you out – a lesson in anatomy. They'll see your insides through your outside – dissection....

'I've always been a refugee – a little boy from somewhere else....'

'It may be simple, Raul,' Mahnaz says. 'Remember, not to trust, no one's to be trusted, not anyone: and certainly – you don't go. You run. How did they know, how did they stick a name on you....? Can you be sure it wasn't me? How can you make a plan when you are vulnerable? And terrified?'

'There's states that's jackals, Mahnaz, even hyenas,' I say. 'They're always there, but there's no one over them now....'

'For sure, your forest burned,' she says. 'It used to be the witches' home it started from – now, it's the trees, they go, and then your hut, the animals, the cats, they crowd in to your space, and you're not there.'

'No,' I say. 'I'm in the prison, with the police. Some, even many, do survive. You can't give up, and hope for quick oblivion, because inside – it's arbitrary.'

'If your friend, Khalil, arrives,' says Mahnaz, 'we'll all see fear. Intelligence is always strange, yes – and arbitrary too. It's all laid down, there's rules for what they do – except, you never know.... That's why we've taken out our policies....'

'You mean,' I say, 'you're lovers of the bosses here? Big well-fed guys – they lie on you, they break your ribs – not many think to give a gift. Heavy people – they're no guarantee, but they fall heavier, and being broad, you hide behind them, when they fall – they make a crash, and for a while there's silence. That's what you thought I'd be ... hushed. And – hope....'

'Yes, hope,' she says. 'That should be good. That I want, and pushing guys like you, promoting them, choosing who is promising, and likely to be fingered first: liberated, perhaps, or banged up, hung up by your toes or sold or rented out....'

'It's not at all what I had thought an expedition did,' I say.

*

There's dogs: in marked packs – three-card tricks. Now you see them, now you don't.... Barking mad – they'll have your guts, your wallet. Dynasties, hierarchies, black dogs, red dogs, yellow dogs, all after us.

The bus stops on the highway, won't go into town ... those narrow streets.... It tries rushing past – they fear a hold-up.

'Give me your sword,' says Mahnaz. 'You can't take it on board.'

It's a tulwar, made in a local smithy, clumsy, unbalanced – it's like the one my father gave me. 'The grip is tiny, Mahnaz,' I tell her. 'Even your hand's not small enough....'

'They're all like that,' she says. 'The soldiers were all much smaller then. Everyone believed the same. They didn't worry about death, they thought it was so temporary....'

I find a stave: we stand out in the road – the bus is grey-blue, a bolt, the slipstream throws us together as it careens past, nearly hitting us, and Mahnaz pulls away from me – 'Not an embrace....' I say, to reassure her. Maybe not true....

'Go, go!' she shouts – the bus has stopped a kilometre down the road, it's clear I'm not a threat, it waits for me. I chase. It's full – the passengers – their faces stone, cycladic masks. They eat foods unknown to me – jellies big as rubies, peacock thighs. Sometimes they sing. They came into this land on horseback, camels, donkeys, and on foot. Now, they run, it's normal, they escape, they're off, invading somewhere else.... By bus.

*

I don't speak their language, so I have my memory, sit and turn it over....

*

'Our new religion,' Mahnaz said, 'is fear. All religions started so. Some fear the apocalypse – but we know there's something more concrete: not a virus, nor a flood, nor famine. Fear, walking in front, behind us, in our shoe, our knickers – making us powerful, making us sneaky, making us inept. It has priests, no icon: it's our face, red, white, in the glass.

'We've left the fields. Let those fend for themselves. Maybe the deserts will grow green wings while we're not there to tramp and chivvy them. Into the towns we go, all piled in, pack into the little rich houses with our bundle, take out the furniture, we, refugees, we'll use the carpets and the hangings as our blankets.... Me – I'm not me. I'm in transition, seeing what I must be next, whatever, whoever asks me. It could be fine – enlightenment, with revolution, end of slavery, all heaped on ... then, into the unknown. Or it could be terrible – revolution, the end of slavery, enlightenment – directory, consulate and empire, the Great Army massacring, defeat, occupation, purges, deportation and internment. Restoration of the great fear.

'Don't miss me. Who are you? Can I use your name, Raul? Were you tenderness – or just more fear? Running – your head made you run, your legs were shackled – don't blame me, I didn't care.... I still don't, can't wait to forget you, forget I exploited you, and how you clung on to me, a leech, a sucker....'

*

It's very easy, everyone expects it's what I'll do. After the bus, I pay, and I am free.

I said I'd no money? It wasn't true, evidently. Or – it was true, and the rest is all a lie. Maybe I stole?

Who carries that much cash?

I'm out, that's all.

*

THE INTERROGATION

Who found the house to sleep in? Sami found it, the house with the sacks of onions. 'The magic mountain of the lachrymose,' he says. 'Onion tears. This is the cure. We're comrades – not in arms; in ships invisible, doing the trip to Troy again. We'll roar, bend trees – find allies. Spar on the shore – try out our Stukas and our drones, our hacks and thrusts. You're Achilles – you'll be stuck here.... I'll be Odysseus: I love witches. I don't ask questions – pigs, witches, dogs, disloyal wives – they're all the same to me. I shall come through. You and I – we're heroes of our time. Most people here – are heroes. Stay or flee – it's all heroic when you'll lose whatever happens. If you run you're heroic. Desert? It's better still.

'There's a cause – not Helen – honour. Slippery. There's no model, no literature, we're up against force, organised – that doesn't need a rule, a law. If you've enough force, prepared to use it – a knife against a club, a gun against a knife – you don't need justify ... Sit on a horse? inside? that's made of tin, perhaps, a stink-bomb in its bowels, ingratiates and wheedles, an installation, infrastructure project, and you're changed! Your word. What is that worth? Honour – where is it worn? On your hat or on your prick...?'

'Why honour?' I ask.

'It's a neglected theme,' he says. 'It's naff. It stinks. It's invisible – that's what we'll end with. You don't get medals if you run away – only if you are an athlete on the track and run towards.'

'It's our new religion, like they say,' he carries on. 'It's *us*: Take dinosaurs – they could evolve, but good and evil, Eve and Adam – they weren't in their range. Eat, sleep and sex – no moral moil and toil. So God got tired, and wiped them out. A thunderbolt.

'Started again with us – maybe we evolve, but we evolve the bad that's much much stronger than the good. Each thing we invent – the bad side trumps the good. What will we get – a thunderbolt? A cough? A roasting, or a sluice? Our nature – lost its divinity: we lost the horse – we ate her, stuffed our ottomans with mare's hair,' he carries on. 'It's glued our leather moccasins with glue made from her hooves....'

'You're inventive, Sami,' I say, quite enviously. 'But you're lachrymose. You've found your resting place....'

'This is where we give each other medals, Raul,' he says.

Is this another relationship, I wonder. 'I'd tell you how I got here, Sami, but how I've voyaged – these countries aren't like what you might expect,' I say. I feel I need to give an explanation. I say, 'There's peeling rooms and fences, it's not like on the map, the colours everywhere the same, the space is tiny and policed ... there's people who betray you, people who point – up to God, or over to a safe place where you can huddle till it's dark. I'd take a shelf of texts to tell it all – Simplicius, who starts a simple runner, then becomes more wily, wondering what will remain.... Not people, obviously – in good times, they're evanescent, all disappear in any situation – no, it's the set-up that another crew will find, when they pretend to fly the ship, and plot its course. The globe – squashed grapefruit shape – that is the given, you just skate round, you navigate, you blast off, but it's home, you are an earthling even in the sky.... You don't go anywhere. Your head, gravity is rooted there, it is your world, your grapefruit. The signs don't tell you if it's Mars or Venus, or a matrimony between them both – the signs say Quine and Tarski, Godel, witty Witters ... all crewmen who fell out the diligence, the dirigible ... took the reins, and fell off the coachman's box....'

He stares at me. 'Egypt?' he asks. 'That's where you were, where the dig began? Lands of the black pharoahs, Assyrian charioteers – and the big library, burnt, or lost, gone under? The names, they could be anywhere ... Mahnuz-Mahnaz? The journeys end and end, the obstacles repeat, low mountains, high rivers, waves and nets – it disappears, but it's still there ... the documents, interrogators, then the dust.... there are maps. Dig, sieve, find yourself, your bones, your father's bones when he was an infant lad.

'They'll catch you, trap you by a leg, they dig you out: the inquisitors.

'The books you read – they read you.... The unread books? More dust. You're free of them, they're just benevolent, you'd think. Dust to dust. It blows around, the walls fall down, there's dynamite and age, old age – powdery cement, turning back to seaside sand, the dust that ought to settle but instead it camps out in your lungs and turns your guts to ox-tail soup. The punishments – undeserved and indiscriminate. Then, anger bubbling out, like liquid methane – every planet made of it, that is the principle. Rage. Not love or fear – you can live with those, watch as they become a bore – but rage is what the universe is built on: the dragon that feeds upon itself and grows and grows, spits blood over your walls and in your eyes.

'No, Raul,' says Sami kindly. 'You don't have the power to sail up to the stars, the thrust to spade the earth: – no commitment, you started bland, with nothing. When you lose your nothing, what have you become?'

'It's always a rehearsal,' I say. 'And the script is always different each time you go on....'

'Your trouble is,' says Sami, 'you're self-important. It's good. But the rest of us, all who you encounter – our inner life doesn't interest you. You're a play with one character, the others stand around until you're done. Like Tsar Ivan – you're terrible until you're dead, always central. Then you die, and you're a virus – all the other Terribles that you infect, measure themselves against your catafalque.

'People are tired of compromise,' I say. 'The old compromises – triple gods, two natures, gods with four, six arms – they don't convince. In the street, no one carries holy books: you're angry. You take your side – throw rocks or lash out with your night-stick, your bullets.... Floods and fires, the prison with the meat-hooks ready.'

'You're shallow, Raul,' says Sami. 'Everybody knows the sky is starry. We all look up, always – it's black. We know there's light up there, the photos tell us so – it's just the light above's invisible: a paradox, we see the dark, the light is hidden. You need look further – where they do things different. The person at your side ... are they from space, its connoisseurs? Or passers-by, who sleep with you, take your cash, have you develop their psychology, and then they're off ... rocket, bus, what do you care how they depart?'

*

'Woe! Woe Russia! (Modest Moussorgsky)

'Here's my advice,' says Sami. 'Russians love jewellery. Give them nothing else. It establishes presence, a complex dependency; and it's saleable – that is the legacy of "Crime and P..." Avoid Americans, they're all sneaks: they shop everybody to their boss.

'As an Arab, I'd say – trust me with your life, but even better, trust a Turk: or an Iranian. And best of all, trust nobody.'

'That's precious, Sami,' I tell him. 'But, I need a chart to steer around.'

'There's parties you could join,' he says. 'Ethnicities – if you can figure what those are....'

'There's risks as well,' I say. 'In those. It's like tattoos. Best have the kind that can wash off. Remember wolves, how they wore sheepskins on the windside of a flock, or trotted round in granny's cloak ... maybe take a hint from them.'

'You'd need a pair of pointy ears,' says Sami. 'Besides, you have a plan. It's not just to pass, inventing something improbable, and dying old. You need to work on it.'

'My plan,' I say, 'I acknowledge – it was childish. Freedom without democracy. No joining, no community, no state. A boss is just a boss, even if you vote for her.'

'They'll steal your teeth, Raul,' says Sami, laughing. 'Quicker than your community, your state. Quicker even than your boss. Other people: your lookalikes. Maybe they'll let you carve on rocks, if you do it in the dark, and under water.'

'No, no,' I say. 'Creative stuff – it is a trap. There is a field of culture, where you reproduce, like geese, laying pot eggs for other geese to brood on, hoping one at least is gold. No, Sami, people are either fachos, trying to steal your land, or else they're democrats who keep you off their fields with guns....'

'It's so,' he says. 'Though even so, you're optimistic: bland and simple. And – why bring the Russians in?'

'I think that's what I am,' I say. 'The name.... The wandering in vast space, coming home unchanged. The choice of suffering, the sacrifice for trivialities....'

'It doesn't prove a thing,' says Sami. 'That's everyone. The only question is "who whom" – and all the rest is folklore. As for names – we all choose the one that fits. The places too, where we're from, where we're going....'

'What are you, Sami?' I ask him, and settle back.

'If they conscript you, don't resist,' he says. 'Show intelligence, end in Intelligence. Like me. You're in security. People are adaptable, or else you founder. The sleeker you swim on – the more the scams you get to do – you personalise the plan, the great campaign, to keep your side on top, whatever changes you may make, or undergo.... Be kind, be harsh – be sure you know who is above you, how far you must obey. We in security – react. We block you when we can. And if we don't, we swim along with you.'

'But,' I say. 'The dirty stuff – the hanging up on hooks, the drones, the spying ... I don't know....'

'There's no job,' he says. 'That doesn't disgust – sometimes. You're trained to think of life as precious, unique to every one. You mustn't take that path. You live exactly as

I said: you are not precious, you are not a gem, there's no intrinsic worth in you, in anything.... We're all the same, and if the others don't agree, so much the worse for them....'

'And it's more work for you....' I finish off for him. 'My friend Khalil – he dodged conscription, but he's ended up like you, punishing what doesn't fit, and isn't right – maybe he's risked more, maybe ... his work – it sounds like yours, except it's more decisive, riskier....'

'I'm sure he'll find a way,' says Sami, sooothing me. 'Security. That is the aim. Then – if it all falls down, it's history; with luck we shan't be there....'

*

We watch the waves. A boat, full of struggling fish, pulls in. The cheerful sailors lay out the fish – all slick and fine, 'Vigorous', says Sami. 'Full of life – big ones too, like battle-cruisers.... A bang on the head for each. And it's done. No regrets from the catchers, none from the boilers, broilers, roasters, and the devourers.'

'Yes,' I say. 'At the abattoir, you can protest. Those landscapes in your head – the randy shepherdesses and the lusty swains, the woolly joints a-baa-ing; flocks waiting for the massacre, the cleansing.... Europa – seated on the ribs and brisket.... At the fishery – no one declaims: not yet. You suffer in silence, and the fish – they thrash and grasp ... there's not time to intervene, no pity, no soft death, no swift.... Life has stopped before it's conceded to them: that humane reflection, shining the second before life ends. The pigs, the sheep ... some are stoic, some ask "why", some beg.... It's no good: too bad, too late. The work, the aftermath: the butchering – it isn't pleasant, not the best ... and surely not paid well. But fish – they haven't learnt. They don't ingratiate, don't ask. They know – they're used to being eaten by their brothers ... it's been set up that way, there is no other. They just gasp, and then – into the pot ... the fire. Not a tear....

'They say the lobsters....' I begin. Then I realise.... I remember, the parable ... their tears, the armour shrieking ... how they begged for cooler waters, the pleading ... only got them a hotter fire ... ah! the hope, the vanity – produces such suffering....

'Order, Raul,' he says. 'Not left or right. No politics, no ethic, no morality. Order is everything, it's the eternal return we have to hope for.... You imagine: with fish, you might have a choice. Extermination, and you go on to another depth – molluscs or denizens. Or else: you try to maintain the stocks, hunt intelligently, with moderation. You are cautious: the fish – have time, have luck, they reproduce, they have a cycle – life without a human hunger....'

'I understand, Sami,' I say. 'I'm grateful. You want to educate me, justify yourself, and save me from the dangers – more, my naivety, my mistakes. Every system rests on the repression it calculates and practices.... If it is not orderly, it fails – doesn't maintain its structures, territory, loses an army, faces jacqueries.... To maintain its order, naturally – it uses drones and gas and tanks – in moderation. If not – extermination: as they say, you today, and me tomorrow. Moderation, like excess, turns out, often, sometimes, a disaster. Counter-productive....

'But I don't believe you, my dear friend,' I go on. 'Keeping order – it's a privilege, and you, Sami, you have benefit from it. It's your job: do what you wish and don't be scrutinised.... Or else the calculation needed to establish order is your fantasy.... There is no plan – there's instinct, for survival, or for self-esteem. Order is chance, a little skill and blunder; and repression when it serves. You set the price of bread too low, to feed the towns. The peasants can't live so poor, you confiscate the flour, coerce, there's dearth, the farmers eat the grain held back for sowing the next year, and there's famine, deportation, armed resistance – more confiscation: famine for everyone. That's the story. No plan, no order. You or them. Or both.'

'You have to realise, Raul,' he says, 'if you are for any reason on the other side to me – you must be very very careful that you win. If you contest – don't lose! It's much much worse than suffering injustice.... It's friendship makes me warn you. Order is one thing: not ending in the net or on the hook ... is quite another.'

'Your friendship is another thing again,' I say. 'Not a warning, not resistance: friendship's a tepid word! Maybe I may like you – what does it mean? Can you believe in friendship of that kind – and what could it involve? Sacrifice? Or sex? With you, or someone close, or bought? Taking a shine to someone, tipping a wink? Drinking together? Going on the dodgems, hunting deer?'

'You're right to be a sceptic,' Sami says. 'Since I could hand you in.'

'Maybe we'll eat the fish until they're gone,' I say. 'Then we'll all eat something else. It's no big deal.'

*

'Try me out, Sami,' I say. 'Suppose I'm at your disposal. What do you say? You wouldn't hurt me, surely...?

'You'd talk. You like that, Raul,' he says. 'I should encourage you. The more you talk, the fiercer you become, the more – up comes your childhood, the first lessons of how to behave, why you ignored them, what to believe and why you stopped, and why you don't know ... not anything, you say, but really, you don't recognise ... not me, my picture, my world, not my or anyone's intelligence, only your own ... and always in your eyes green fields, in your ears: singing birds....

'We'd meet quite often, and you'd talk. You'd not contest, propose – just show that really, you're no use. You're irreconcilable, a feather – gets up people's nose and irritates the brain. A joke, a pleasantry, a play on words that everyone finds boring, but insistent.

'Then, we don't meet so often. A month will pass, and I'm distracted, I don't listen. 'What have I done wrong?' you think. 'My logic, my invention, anger, superiority, contempt – what effect have they not had?'

'Let a year pass. You know you're worthless: no one cares. You're dull – worn through.'

'Yes, that's terrible,' I say. 'You haven't touched me, I'm still a cloud of starlings. I'm irreducible, irreconcilable. You'd better kill me, bury me in that arid patch....'

'It's where you have belonged from when we locked your door,' he says. 'It is your home. You've been an intellectual, a hero, explorer, friend of the friendless, apostate – a guru no one hears or sees.... Your life – it's not been bad, except the end, when you asked me to interrogate you.... But earlier – no crap jobs, no poverty, no loss of an identity ... always the storm-cock and the lark, the nightingale – and at the end, the wise old owl, maybe.'

'And they pay you, Sami, to talk to me?' I ask. 'I could do that!'

'I told you,' he says. 'I'm your friend.'

Keep on the move. If you settle somewhere – you'll dangle. If you have a job – or many jobs, or the many you might take if they would ask – it's never nearly adequate, and it's never certain. If you stray – you end with someone like a Sami, who may not be your friend.... Or you might get hurt some other way: working, walking around ... by a mistake. Best move for ever in wide arcs, find somebody who's interested in you, puts you in a show, an interview, a book, a video, a leaflet, takes you on an expedition, feeds you....

I think –

'I should find other people, lots – not quite like me, but who might put me in a frame ... for safety.'

*

'I can make your name,' says Cendrine. 'But I'll take half. You were lucky to find me....'

'Not really,' I say. 'I looked for you everywhere.'

Looked for someone with a jersey suit in grey, who'll get me cash and interviews.

'The book,' she says. 'It won't take me long. Two weeks. You've invented all your life yourself. Your lover's death –

the music, then the digging holes. It's logical. The singing. Terror, soldiering – escape. The wandering after prison. Then – the interrogation: it has shape. Life, Raul! Does yours have life? Or is it merely every life – a dud. A fake. Diving in shoals of other people, tracks feet-beaten, air re-breathed. You can't survive all that and feel, consider, experience ... be novel ... pretend you're individual. That is the point. To communicate, you must disappear, become another bubble in the fizz....'

'I could come out wise,' I say. 'But that means silence. No use if you're on show.'

'When we're on camera,' she says, 'I'll look at you – unrelenting and concerned. They'll think we're lovers.'

'What do you want it all to mean, Cendrine?' I ask. 'You've left out Mahnaz....'

'That was your escape,' she says. 'It's boring, inconclusive. If you want, go back, start off again – maybe the bus, it didn't stop, and you're still waiting on the road. Mahnaz is our sequel. Maybe I could be her, grow into her. I am sneaky. I've told you, I take half of what you are, and I could be your better half, a Mahnaz....'

Hers is a short book, the biography of me myself. I embody transcendental homelessness. That's quite correct, it is the protocol. In fact, I long to have a home, someone apart from me who loved me for myself. It wasn't so. I floundered. I confess – I knew terrorists, admired their determination, their stupidity, their being unlike me: implacable, destructive. Doomed, false, death-bearing.... They trusted books, so much it became, by logic, one book that witnessed everything. Instead of you speaking to it and throwing it down – it did exactly that to you. It seems I took drugs, was converted, changed countries, was captured.... All nonsense. A buffalo! as the Italians say.

'Talk to the sharp lady,' Cendrine says. 'Confess to me. You'll become an actor, so you're cleansed of who you were. The cops don't watch this, it's full of laughs at what aren't jokes.... It's like Vienna if the emperor hadn't died and they'd not built the Engels Hof, if Benjamin was for ever on the panel, vatic and meandering. Take courage! Their job is to make you seem of interest, and appear stupider than you are. Help them, and laugh....'

*

Oh Cendrine! ... if only.... Our music – we could have made some. Nothing like Fatimata, just a strum and hum. Her world – one of good behaviour: they stab you in the back, not in the eye. She smells of stuff you buy, stuff made by someone else. What's she like? She's in the fashion, all bought in – you can't describe her, after a week, it's all moved on, she too....

*

Jeanne, the smart lady, asked me, 'These episodes you went through – what do they signify, what do they teach...?'

'She isn't supposed to ask,' says Cendrine. 'You said your boundary fence was made of deaths and memories, Raul. What's in the paddock you have made? Buzzing things, creatures that climb from holes.'

'I should have said – times and space. Times without figures on the dial, and spaces without age,' I say.

'You have to die,' says Cendrine. 'That way you have a shape – eliminating time and space – what's left would be your quiddity.'

'But to me – it is invisible. The shape,' I say. 'The End: is written, comes up on the screen – that way the fence is made complete, annealed, an area of change and travel's circumscribed. It's all a fraud,' I say. 'Death gives us weight, authority – a trip is done. And – you're not there, not there to tell the tale.'

'Life is not for you, Raul,' she says. 'If you're religious – then, maybe. So – it's up to whoever studies you, not that they benefit, become wise – you're not a soul, you are an article: a sucked gobstucker, lifts for a shoe, a padded bra, false eye, a trumpet for the angel, trumpet for your ear.... You're an invention, a character, not as interesting as some, not full of complexity, like a cheese, a shoe, that's full of holes.'

'I've had my transformation, Cendrine,' I say. 'My addiction first. Then there were the prisons – small rooms. I'm a cabinet of curiosities: escaping from unlikely credences: unsuitable and sterile partnerships ... skating on the earth as if it's made of glass....'

'Read my book,' says Cendrine. 'It's your book, your life. It tells what's in your paddock – those elephants and tigers, dug up, wound up – set shambling on the ice – the key to life as it was, as it will never cease to be.... The habitus, Raul – produces monsters, teeny things, cinders and snow, and we are them, and something quite ridiculous, between the big and small ... the lithe, the slack ... the gullible, the bullying ... we wave the flags, indifferent, like chimps with fronds – black flags, red flags....

'You can't say it's love you want.... You wouldn't recognise it, besides, it wouldn't last, you are not full, you're mostly empty, save for a smear of pepper paste, steel balls that roll and rattle – can't do sex.... Mathematics knows no solid and no circular ... those must be ball-bearings, dropped from Ashoka's wheel, or asteroids, detritus spun off still spinning....'

'It's not me,' I say. 'That is your book. You're the one that's closed in it. I....'

'You're enclosed,' says Cendrine. 'You wanted civilisation, and it has you in its jaws. So – what's different? The chance to own or be a slave: it's still out there. It's Chance, not Choice. What choice is that, to do what you didn't want to do, to have what you couldn't use?'

*

'Puff me up, Cendrine,' I tell her. 'Make me interesting. Clean me out, so I can see where I have been and start again.'

*

'They were more interested in you than me,' I say, when I have appeared and disappeared again.

'Of course,' says Cendrine. 'Jeanne, her lover Tilda – they collect souls. The book is mine, and you're in there, I squeezed your cortex, all the juice flowed out. You are nowhere. You need another soul – I thought that's what you want. What has happened so far – it's inconclusive – you've been too pressed to have a personality. I gave you one ... invented ... prudent, a spectator.... But – you immersed in everything and trusted everyone....'

'I told you everything,' I say. 'You stole it. And it's just that people prefer a biography to someone real, who in any case – they'll never see.'

'People want a show,' she says. 'If you don't give it, they'll put salamanders in your shoes and paprika patties in your pants – humans want to see high kicks and hear your lamentations.'

*

Jeanne's house is full of tricks ... mobiles and porn and miniatures – food and temples painted, tiny in aluminum.... She moves round her guests: she doesn't love them, not anyone. We are quite a bore.

Her helper, Diomede, says to me, 'It was right the Bolsheviks should try to build a future land. It was an experiment to be tried, but never more. It was a project, gigantic, to end them all. Instead, when it had failed, the others took it up. Cleansing, religion, cults of nobodies.... They still go on. It can't be done, and there's no way to stop....'

'Jeanne would set up the French Revolution,' says Karol, Diomede's friend. 'Talk out and over all its variations. After a week, no one would want to proceed with it. Then she'd sacrifice her lamb, Tilda, and afterwards, no one would try to change the bump and grind of everyday....'

'Oh, Karol!' says Diomede, almost giggling. 'Jeanne might sacrifice you....'

They laugh, they're very close. It's hard to talk to them, they're there to ask the questions, but Karol is right. The revolutionaries talk, correct the line, take their revenge, insist – and Jeanne would hear them out. And then it's done. The king and queen are headless, dead – but all the rest is cancelled out. There's gaps, but nothing to regret....

*

I wait to hear the question, 'Raul! What do you do in life?' but no one asks. I've had my turn, been interviewed, invented a life motto.... 'Earned eternal rest.'

'Away, away,' says Cendrine, pulling me.

'Wait!' says Tilda. 'Jeanne wants to know – why did you do what you did to get to here?'

'Jeanne doesn't seem powerful,' says Cendrine. 'She questions, doesn't want the answers.... Raul told her all he remembered. Not conclusive, naturally. She didn't stop the revolutions either, just rewrote them here and there....'

'It's not stopping anything that she's after,' says Tilda. 'It's so you can go on, pretend nothing ever happened except her.'

'I wasn't interested in me,' I say. 'It was to find the regularity. I knew then I'd be safe.'

'And if there's none?' asks Tilda.

'That's what I hoped,' I say. 'Searching. That way I'd be safe.'

'Being safe – it's so important to you?' Tilda asks. 'You were all set to be a leader, commander. Your Mahnaz – prepared you for a perilous life – and you said "no". More perilous still, that is your wish....'

'It's not important,' I say. 'Safety? It's a given. I can make it so. I have reason on my side, my head. There is nothing more.'

They laugh. It's my best joke, ever!

*

'"The influence of Sufism on the construction of monumental complexes in Inner Asia" – I have that down as your interest, Raul,' says Tilda, frowning at a piece of paper.

'That was the subject. I used it to apply for funds,' I say. 'It's a title.'

'There was your cloistering, all the time until you took the bus,' she goes on.

'The world is full of leaders. The more democratic it's supposed to be, the more leaders there spring up. Mahnaz had some idea.... I'm sure I had the qualities. I refused, refused the manacles,' I say.

'The responsibility?' she asks. 'For what you might have done?'

'Responsibility without punishment? Apologies for your disasters? Does a reminder help? That's having to remember – "feed the cat with the canaries". Passion – close your eyes, relax, surrender – sweet and sickly. Remember – don't mention the Cheka – no one does, you needn't, everyone knows it's there ... the story.'

'We'll have to make you legendary,' Tilda says. 'In view of where you're going to go.'

'That's a gambit Tilda,' I say. 'It was a struggle, humans becoming individuals. I think the starting point was horses – when we broke the horses in the spring, and freed them in the winter – every year the same. And we were individuals. We made a pact with horses, free or broken, and there was, symbolically, a pact with nature on the same terms – subjugation, then a separation ... but not, never, one between individuals.

'Then, we were closed, voluntarily, in societies. Miserable for what we'd lost – the horses and our individuality....

'The infinite universe, Tilda – is that a further problem? Is that nature, or something absolutely different, in which we're lost.... Indifferent to us, no pact?'

'No, Raul,' Tilda says. 'We're never lost. You should be grateful to Cendrine. She took your wandering, made it a story, and so it looked as though it had a meaning ... as if it was a part of history. You draw on walls, I bet. Respect the pitches of the others, your rivals, painters, carvers ... patrons ... the shamans of all stripes.... It all starts up again, the game: the pieces in the box are standardised – the games are infinite, of course ... but it's all there: pride, bullying, the ethics and the copying.... The boundaries are set.'

'I don't have a story, Tilda,' I tell her. 'The story Cendrine made – was something alien. I owe her nothing.'

'I'm only joking,' Tilda says. 'We – Jeanne and I – each day we read the stories, see the people, breakers of populations, signers of every pact, breakers of every horse. You have all the time you want to explain yourself to everyone. Ten minutes. It's abundant – in that time, you're quite bled out. And – nothing! Most don't hit the gold, don't hit – don't even see – the target.'

'Living in society – is sacrifice,' I say. 'It's compassion, naturally.... Suffering. Makes you a doctor, sometimes; sometimes a murderer.'

'Don't try to go too deep, Raul,' says Tilda. 'Everything is surface – that is physics! Think, rather – those expeditions: what do you carry with you and pretend you've found it somewhere?'

'Alas, it all depends,' I say. 'Sometimes, I bring authority, the structure, the end, the lesson; sign off as mister death. Sometimes – I think it is the contrary – I bring awareness, transcendent possibility, instruction, hypothesis, alternative existences....'

'It doesn't matter,' Tilda says. 'Try to decide. That is what matters.'

'I bring my end,' I say. 'But know that I am infinite. The questioning is infinite, and until a better species comes along – repetitive. The answer? – I suspect it's trivial. A closed hole, a spurt of dust. End. Someone else's turn.'

*

'My curiosity, Tilda,' I say. 'You're all quite sharp – but have faces dull and formulaic. The secret's in your shirts....'

'Exactly,' Tilda says. 'Diomede's beard is grizzled-grey, and Karol has a topknot, amber teeth. Jeanne's tobacco colour, and I'm quite black. You know who's who, but that is not enough. They give us each a t-shirt with a portrait or a quote – you spend the time in figuring....'

'Who you're all supposed to be....' I finish for her.

'Like you, Raul, we have a problem of our destination,' Tilda says. 'Where we go, how long we have – the general survival, and how long each of us is current ... pertinent. The world is like a rocket, not a platform – a rocket full of millions – as it slows and gyres – millions drop out the open doors, to keep us going on we may need steersmen, painters, engineers – the rest can keep on dropping into space....'

'Mahnaz thought I was an inspiration for multitudes – she was wrong,' I say.

'There's lots have cash or beauty, a turn of words, an old-fashioned job – but nothing counts. Faster, we travel into the dark: the thrust – it finished long ago. It's physics; and the pieces falling off – how do you prepare for that?' she asks.

*

'You trusted Cendrine, Raul,' says Tilda. 'She made our task much easier – but probably you were naive.... Cendrine's a bridge: in order to exist, she needs two shores.'

'She did what I asked her....' I begin.

'That's the worst of trust,' says Tilda. 'And of friends. Being talkative and innocent – those do not help.... Everything you told her went to us, she worked for us, and we had more than everything to put you on the files....'

'I've done nothing, Tilda – even more – done nothing wrong,' I say.

‘Well,’ she says. ‘Those expeditions show your innocence.... It’s neutral. Digging things up – it almost always means you find dead things, or stuff that’s thrown away, forgotten, or destroyed. But – there’s Khalil. If he comes here, they’ll bang him up. For life, maybe. And if he tries to contact you, they’ll arrest you both, or find some other way to make you hurt....’

‘Khalil wanted a good time....’ I say. ‘Not soldiering....’

‘Well,’ Tilda says. ‘He’s fighting now. Aziza’s plotting – her compound’s full of politicians, waiting for their turn. Mahnaz – she’s looking for your double – a substitute, who’ll mobilise; gather a camel corps, a horde of horses, ride on, on to destruction. Alas, she’s a poor destiny – we gave the news of everyone to Sami, and he has told us details you are certain to deny....’

*

Tilda’s quite at home – she sprawls on a divan that started grey and now is brown.... Here is not a bar and not a club, there’s rooms that go far back, with brocade, with lino, and with winceyette ... there’s tables where they play the shell game, Monopoly with title deeds ... the guys communicate with messages in tubes on wires, that flash across the room on air that’s been compressed, encrypted – vacuums you shouldn’t fill and plots you shouldn’t cultivate....

‘Tilda,’ I say. ‘This is a thieves’ kitchen, but there’s nothing cooked – lots to drink, nothing to eat except those salted herrings with a mustard sauce....’

'Of course we do research, Raul,' she says. 'Your life is not just as you tell us. Now, it is public, even if it's hidden from you.... Your friends – you loved them, trusted them, and ran from them – did you suspect they are a locust storm that starts to chirrup and to chirr...? And did you do or pass in silence anything they asked you to and maybe seemed quite fun and necessary – all the constraints, the projects, did you go along with those, as though you were a traveller arriving on a foreign world...?'

'If I had known, Tilda,' I say. 'I'd see it all quite different. I have a world view based on understanding, curiosity.... Detail isn't me.'

It's true. It's not *entirely* true.

'Oh Raul,' she says, and laughs. 'We gather information – we don't judge! Like you – we want to know, find patterns, regularities, the purpose and direction of it all....'

'You've seen my life,' I say. 'What does it tell?'

'All those extremists that you know,' she says, slipping her arms through mine. 'Exotics too! Of course – we're all extremists now, and disclaim exoticism – but underneath – we shimmer! We experiment!'

She pushes me behind a screen – it would be the kitchen, but there's nothing there but boxes – 'finnan haddies' and the like, barrels of mustard from Cremona and Dijon – 'My! You're a weedy type,' she says, pulling off my clothes. 'I'll soon have done with you, and change your image too – the next time, you'll figure as the little male who's sacrificial, I can have you filleted, and dip you in the can of peppy joy that's here ... consume ... enjoy ... if necessary, spew and separate....'

They look like shelves – they're narrow bunks, where once you might have taken pipes – 'Chop chop!' says Tilda. 'No lingering!'

She starts to do the dance, she struts, and flaps, and turns a camera on, puts a grebe crown on her head – there is no rival to impress but on she prances – and I say, 'Dear Tilda, you convince me – you are beautiful and strong and full of sexual confabulation – but are you certain you want fledglings ... and the mess, the shells, the children ... How they demand! They harry you – and there's the hawks.... And just to set me up, to make a reputation I don't want ... the drab, the nondescript, the postulant who doesn't beg and doesn't strut.'

'Look!' she says, holding out a long brown arm, 'I'm speckled.' And she is. 'Don't be afraid,' she says. 'The intercourse? It's substance, without meaning or significance. It's glue. You make it out of skeletons – these fish; just boil the bones up, and when two human bodies lie, side by side, or on top or any way you can imagine – you take a trowel and smarm it on. The skins, they stick. Some never come apart, but most – are marquetry. The chips, the squares and slivers, slacken: fall. Mating – it's quite instinctive: like what you've come through, grooming and imprisonments, and didn't ruffle you, not a bit, and so I know – you have no goal, you're sceptical; an apostate. Like me, you do not judge, do not reflect, don't hold a grudge, a memory. You know the history. Everybody can do anything. They have, they will, and they will justify or plead, deny, condemn and take revenge. Pain, Raul, is built in to our system – cause or effect, inflict or suffer – you just flip the switch: our seven deadly virtues, deadly sins, they're on the panel of control ...

like vengeance, pardon, indifference and ignorance. Each has an armoury identical: each one of us lines our brothers, sisters, up along the ditch, sometimes we topple them, sometimes we make them priests and pom-pom girls....

'Your trouble is – you're in your skin. You can't be other; what you are is what we are – perfidious humanity, the sneaky species, who invented traps and poison snares. You would desert, Raul, like Khalil thought he would, but then he got the sting, the prick ... he caught belief, the faith, obedience – the fear ... belief is just as easy as your disbelief, forward is easier than back. It's like you found: when a room has doors and locks, a little window high – you find the guy who will fit in there, and when he's been inside a while, he will have thought of everything that justifies him being trapped and paying back if he gets out ... like you were held: for not believing anything at all....'

'It isn't so,' I say. 'Tilda! You lock us up and steal our prints, the patterns of our hair, our wrinkles and our sags, you prize our crimes, invent some more.... You are our writers, our creators: we are your characters, inventions ... your shadows....'

'Oh no!' she says. 'How dull you are! You're moving on to crimes! And good and bad! And sides, and what you are and wish you weren't. I'm not responsible for that, for any of it. Our – my – interest's in what you'll do, that's all. I'm just a pawn; I'm Alice, just a step from toppling the queen ... and being one.'

'My compliments,' I say. 'Jeanne is dead, checkmated. But – in the game I know, there's lots of kings, and queens. They coexist; or else you might cut off a head....'

'In my game,' Tilda says. 'There's room for only one of any kind....'

'You're wrong,' I say. 'It's true you think I am a solitary – but we all come from the one place. We are all Maghrebini – some trekked in from Egypt, some were Vandals, others Fatimids, we spread out South and East and North. We're all the same, identical. Not hybrids, not of anything – we're standard issue. We fit in everywhere ... Macao and Sakhalin....'

*

When we leave, I look out for the sign. I'd like to come back, be a member, client ... a diplomat, elected bomber ... go with them to torch some buildings, sit on the ladder, helmeted, as on we race to put out fires.... I see 'HOT FOOD', but there's no door, just a machine in its place, like one that used to give out ciggies, even that self-heating soup the American soldiers dropped on Vietnam.... That licence has expired, so anyone can use it anywhere....

I must come back and do a proper search.

'We're not communicators, Raul,' says Tilda. 'Our show – it doesn't matter. It's all the rest we operate: we run this place, know everyone, and all the topics ... what will happen.... Telling people? – it's not our thing. We know – that should be enough for anyone!'

'I know you'd say that, Tilda,' I say. 'My dead friend, Claudia – she said, "One person can reveal it all – the mechanism, structure, what was and what will be. You think it's complicated – maybe it is, but one small head can work it out."'

*

'I guess I always knew more than I let on – it puts you in a perilous place, and doesn't help you, not at all,' I say. 'Tilda – you don't engage, you bewilder. I'm curious. But – curiosity – must it lead to more bewilderment?'

'Being beat up by cousins on your first date?' says Tilda, and she scoffs. 'Watching on TV the tanks come down your street and pointing at your door? ... The creepy movie; sat upon the throne, Jack Horner eating sugared eye-balls from a poke.... That's what made you? Stock encounters? You were amazed, surprised: it hurt! Losing those limbs, finding those bodies on the stairs? Everyone you'd known? Awake! Your ticket's expired. That show is done. Here comes the next! – "Art is dead": now the hero is released, walks off the screen, the page, and pokes a broomstick up your arse. What more can you want, invent? You need a full bio if you want reality to give you work. The girl next door has learned to use her snicker-snee to cut off heads. You're stupid, Raul. Expeditions were the safest place, you blew it, went down into town, befriended giants and maggots....'

'Well, Tilda,' I say. 'It's true, my first world fell on to someone's plate. Take me into your new atlas, make me a star....'

'Oh,' she says, and laughs. 'Star? You're a grey rock. We don't see you till you fall and burrow deep into the dust.

Imagination never got the power ... and the real is all imagined now. Get used to it, and get used to when it's gone.

'Your friends, you didn't know them. They didn't love you. They wanted to share what you had, and create everything they'd want....'

'I know,' I say. 'The courtyards, peach and almond ... the breezes ... where on earth...?'

'Create....' she goes on. 'But had no idea what their want would be. Freedom and justice, those came in. They didn't ask you for your take on those....'

'There wasn't much left of anything to take,' I say. 'Though, they were potent friends. Me ... I went along. They never looked like making it – nor like breaking me.... I'm willow.'

'I'm fixed,' says Tilda. 'And so, I can know things written down, know what's beneath my feet. The lignite pit – if you dig down, you'll find us – layered like lasagna, or moussaka. Civilisations, humans clothed, protected – in furs, then hoplites, centurions, barbarians, then more barbarians, then infidels, miscredents and miscreants, then toffs in uniforms and guys in rags – all fossils, killed by one another.... Forget the climate, Raul: it was all fratricide, feminicide, infanticide – someone should have called the law ... you're the one who ought to know all that – instead, you ran. By running you can learn materials. How cement falls; down goes a wall intact ... and what blows into chips. What tale to tell to save your life....'

'The present, what you deal in, Tilda – it explodes. You live in a future that you know won't come ....' I say.

'My poor dear,' says Tilda, laughing. 'Your adventures haven't taught you much! You're mired in paradox – the more you – everybody – knows, at least in theory, the more you must believe: take on trust. You're up against the wall of apprehension – the permanence of the imaginary, and the fleeting nature of the real. The real – it skitters, dissolves, is recomposed in sometimes tiny, sometimes immense, new detail, definition, and compression. The imaginary – ah! it withers, but it cannot die.'

'Maybe then,' I say, 'to be immortal, you must not have lived.'

'Exactly so!' she says, 'and yet, and yet... Beware! The brain! Don't forget the brain – there the warthog and the unicorn lie side by side – or,' and she giggles. 'Maybe it's the chimera and the dragon – beasts that perhaps once lived, one real and one – perhaps ... not much. Real, imaginary – both up there, beneath your hair, hemmed in by ears, the running nose, the sucking mouth – all noisy neighbours, prone to colds and much much worse....'

'Where does this lead?' I ask. 'You may know everything about today, and all of us who make it up, but what exactly can you *do*? Are you nothing but a pack of cue-cards? Your science works the best on us believing hayseeds, but what of all the rest? The mass of stuff that won't be tested ever.... Intense lives and precarious work, and over everything the fear, that in a minute it can all be swept away, or burnt, sequestered....'

'That's just stuff, Raul,' she says. 'Don't bother yourself about it all. You need to know about me, Raul. Like I already know about you.

'I'm heavier than you think – some of my bones have lapis cores.' She gestures to a diploma on the wall – 'Aromamastery' – 'It's not an easy course,' she says. 'So hard I never felt like further training. I have a super nose: of course, the setters and the labradors were best, but failed the written test....'

She pauses. I don't laugh: I say, 'That's weak, Tilda.'

'I'm not keen at all,' she says, 'on seeing if you laugh. It's what doesn't amuse that opens up your quiddities.... Well done, straight-face! But if it's love, cash, or contacts that you want – I'll lead you by the nose, and you won't scent a thing ... not till the end. There'll be a waft of wainscotting, a sewer breeze at most....'

'You turn everything around,' I say. 'You have to be inside, to manage that: sometimes you're rat, and sometimes cat....'

'Like you,' she says. 'You never say what you want: if you succeed or fail, if you are victim or controller – if you have an aim, and what it is, and why you choose these people – me included – to promote yourself, while you play the simpleton.'

'That would be to waste the time of everyone,' I say. 'Telling the purpose. People want a story, not to think, to suspect, to turn what they are told inside out ... a sock....

'What could I want, Tilda? I don't want position, money, I have no philosophy, no aim, and we both know – the storm blows unrelenting, all you hope for blows away ... perhaps you will remember that. It's knowledge, Tilda, but it isn't wisdom.'

'That is your distinction, Raul,' she says.

'I'm coherent, Tilda,' I say. 'But – you use your ignorance to get power. You're duplicitous. I'm honest. I've lost my belief in everything except in wisdom: – it eludes me. But the people I have met – they need, they believe; they're wrong, they'll fail, be tricked, but they're consistent – they think in ways based on what should have been, what ought to be, what's possible to construct, whatever it will cost, whoever suffers....'

'That's knowing, Raul,' says Tilda. 'You say you understand it all, so that must mean *my* beliefs, *my* history: all that's a mystery to me, yet it seems clear to you.... Will your talk lead one day to wisdom? It just leads to something else.'

'People have changed,' I say, 'since I went digging first. Maybe Syria showed the world. The suffering – it made us build walls in ourselves ... and then we found that – from the start, it hadn't mattered to us, not a bit. The suffering ... we didn't feel a *thing*. We never had. Knowing that – was it a liberation? We could go on and do exactly what we could. It wasn't much. Of course – the Syrians ... they suffered, lots of them. But that was that. It always is....'

'Don't worry that I'm out to fleece you, Raul,' says Tilda. 'You've nothing that I want. And what's this stuff? – Syria? Hallucination or a metaphor? – just cut it out! It's true though – people changed. They're honest now. They don't care. As for me – I'll betray you – without a hesitation. Watch it!'

*

'Wisdom,' Tilda says, 'comes from reflection – not from new experience, discovery – those bring anxiety. Each discovery opens up the dark that lies beyond. More darkness: ever more. Experience? What did the nest of spies teach you, Raul?'

'Maybe I'd repeat it, but with more enthusiasm, Tilda: something fresh? – that's up to you,' I say, longing for another whirl, fastened firm.'

'Exactly so,' she says. 'Let's visit where you've been, see how it strikes....'

'Bring me joy, Tilda,' I say.

'I've looked you up,' she says. 'Joy's not on your menu. Drop your search. Dumb up....'

'I'm not on a list, Tilda,' I say. 'I've been away....'

'If you're away,' she says, 'it means you are a spy, or fighting in forbidden armies, plotting bad things.... Those women, seeking power ... Mahnaz, Aziza! The Qur'an spoke of unity – why it's not been so. The language and the faith – they haven't worked. God wanted peace – the humans didn't: – they wanted power and profit. There's monsters, Raul, human, very human.... Khalil, your carousing friend – bartered or betrayed – maybe he's a minister. Astrid – that dig, it finished bad. That crew are all beneath the slab, objects for forensic archaeologists.... They all went in the hole....'

There's sand, sand everywhere. The desert, I feel the desert in me.

I weep.

*

'Spectators,' Tilda says. 'It's best – learn to be that. Dry your tears. We all have experience of watching. Spectating, watching the watchers, creating them, putting on a show that opens after *they've* put on a show. Being creative, making the effect, then watching as they watch. That's what I do: I make it happen. I make *them.* I make what they aren't become something that is mine. They smile, they weep – like you. They shout. They come alive, because they're me – I'm the water in the clessidra; the oil, the current, in the lamp. You, Raul ... people will say you intrude, you don't belong – that's true, of course. So what? None of us belongs, not anywhere, there is no space someone has scissored out for us, to paste us into. We're all waiting for the thunder, coming up the hill – Timurids, Napoleon, Manchus – all invisible though you hear the hooves.... Then, there they are, and you're transformed: you're them, or you're their prisoner, and your watch is ended.

'Why were you involved, in Aziza's struggle, why were you a candidate selected by Mahnaz? Why did Sami hang you on his hook, the barb just fitting sweetly in the hollow in your foot, between the tendon and the ankle bone.... That's why the spot for an attachment's there, no doubt – it's ready, like our uterus, ready for Messiahs and big devils.... We're made for certain indeterminate and casual happenings, so ... why were you there, spectator Raul, in someone else's business?'

'It was because they wanted me,' I say. 'What for? To change the story. Bananas, sugar, oil – grow those, your chiefs will conjure forth a class of thieves and hypocrites who'll make you sweat and dance for them. If your economy diversifies, and you have empires full of slaves – some miserables you promote, some you sell off ... and you smile on your compatriots. You need them – they protect you, and you need their work.

‘The people? Yes! They are a weapon. Have them on your side – they can be interesting, talented – they wash your clothes and write your songs, play instruments while you leisured dandies dance quadrilles, and honest burghers cook the books and cure the pox....

‘Justice and freedom – why, you can write books about that, while society runs smoothly on its tram-tracks ... wheels ... and deals. Beware! The nobs are fickle – and they make you fight and kill.... Then the people find they’re back again where they began – conforming and unfree.... That is the history. Reason tells you different, of course, more complicated ... there’s class and capital…. It seems it doesn’t work like that....

‘The best place – to have a look,’ says Tilda, not hearing what I’ve tried to say, ‘A gaze – see! start with this gallery we’re in ... a corridor. A limbo, a something in between two somewheres. It’s darkness, lit by lustred objects, like fireflies in the grass. It’s the past, Raul, all jumbled up. A museum. You contemplate it. Is it beautiful, whatever that might be? Or horrible? That’s easier.’

‘It can’t be true, that all we do is look,’ I say. ‘And so much stuff – it’s newly made, outside, it’s hardly lived, dead so soon, thrown in with all the rest ... And people – so keen to see their stuff curated, tagged and framed – as if there was no destiny outside ....’

'Suppose there is none, Raul,' says Tilda, suddenly cast down. 'Let's hope there is a room here, not set up like a gallery with simulacra, curios ... figurines and coaches, smoky pictures, people could be me, or could be painted ones by you, Raul ... self-centred portraits, still dead lives.... Instead, a room, where drivers sit at journey's done, and sing, tell tales, remember all the horses died along the way....'

'That's heavy, Tilda,' I say, cheering up. 'Tears don't help.'

'Maybe at the end of all these galleries there'll be that comfortable room, an orgy, something mild, that we can watch, or have a fling....'

'They're not a cure, Raul,' says Tilda, quickening our pace, and pulling me along. 'Orgies are competitive, and you have to pay, whether you're starring or just watch. Wait – one day, there'll be machines that suffer more than humans, put on a better show. We'll leave it all to them, and we at last can sing and play, and maybe find the innocence we think we had when we were shooting guys and carrying off their womenfolk....'

'It feels like action, Tilda, but –' I say, 'we only ever watch. We're spectators, like those kids in pantomimes, who went up on the stage to sing a song, and then back to their seats.... And you – you're another Claudia, but a Claudia with a shell.'

'You're getting somewhere, Raul,' she says. 'Everything is normal. People want that things should change. They will. And oh! – remember, I don't fancy you. Not physically. We'll go down the corridor and find the cosy room – but then – go find another partner, please....'.

*

In the corridor, she turns to me – 'It's fortunate you're unattractive. There's no temptation there. I have this fantasy – decapitation. Caravaggio – the murderous artist.... I think especially of Judith, after sex with Holofernes – taking the sentry's sword, cutting the throat, then, taken by the rush of blood, on she goes, and cuts. Cuts! And severs! A general, Raul! Of course, there are no generals today – they're bureaucrats, or politicians – you wouldn't want to touch their greasy underwear.

'I'm sure, her gesture was – a love of purity. And then, poor Caravaggio, crossing the border into Naples ... those were the days! Soft borders everywhere – and all the way – the blood. San Gennaro, his blood that still flows after millennia – it takes a magic touch – and it's fluid, an ordinary miracle.... Is there wisdom here?'

'That's deep, Tilda,' I say. 'The mantis feast! Praying, marriage, sex – unpropitious all of them.... Blood – it is a candle flame for you, I'm sure. Remember those old physiologists – Bichat, Bernard, – the vital impulse, the imperative of life, its flood. What is this, Tilda, for you? Crucifixations, the great red dragon? An affectation, a literary sport, or....'

'You're right, it's deep,' she says. 'And yet – of course it's not. Just dangerous. It's what turns the tourists on. It's the spice that makes the time spent scratching at those dreary canvases seem tolerable... Your mask, your swab! .... the indoor-outdoor paint, grimy, antique ... the flesh, grained like old beef: those rosebud nipples – every nude an adolescent –

hands off! or go to jail ... the oldsters with their browning wrinkles, scars, tree-rings.... Oh, what a bore, Raul. Their silence!

'A whole museum, galleries – full of waxworks, traces of life without a voice ... marionettes, a box of shadow-puppets, everlasting flowers that never lived, representations: a mockery! Even the armour's mute ... no clang, no *Klang*. Scholars talking up the price, rigging the auctions – open another gallery, more masters, now you add the mistresses – and on and on....'

'Be thankful that is not your trade,' I say.

'I do not bring the death,' she says. 'It's life that fascinates me – the blood that starts the longest rivers, the arteries....'

'It's fancy, Tilda; and there's no generals here for you, sex is an optional....' I say.

'Oh tiddle-taddle, Raul,' she says. 'Mine is the oldest fantasy that comes to pass. When we are gone, will robots have exterminatory wars, a suicide – over the edge...?

'What you can't stop, you learn to love. We're courted: death whispers in our ear, inserts its long cajoling tongue ... revenge ... be pure! thrust and cut. Unsheath your penis made of steel, your gender makes no difference, we all have one, a snicker-snee, a *Messer*.... You've been violated, abducted, your soul's for sale: so, vengeance!

'Counter, Raul! Riposte! Serve up a prime cut, a leg, an arm, a joint, an organ quivering and moist ... deck the slab: a pig's head, lamb's tongue, calf's brain....'

'I've thought, Tilda, that creating is the only worthwhile thing – those pictures, manuscripts – the symphonies silent in the folios – what else might count? It's true – creation is sterile. Skins sloughed and hung on bushes. A proof you've lived and calved, got it over with, passed, birthed, moved on....' I say.

'You wouldn't know, Raul,' says Tilda, colouring up her face, glitter and kohl, her wens picked out as scarlet cabochons. 'You don't create. You're slow. There was Khalil – wanting a loyal adventurous friend ... Mahnaz who loved you, ending bad for sure, wanting to build you up, and you slid off.... If that is wisdom – it's a fraud....'

'Now you tell me, Tilda!' I say, much excited. 'I thought it was all gratification, literary talk....'

'Everybody's always ready for an orgiastic break,' she says. 'It's just that most are staid and ugly – no one takes them up....'

She's bright, bright as the morning star.

'I know about these things,' she says. 'Khalil too, and your betrayal. Now, he's hunted like a dingo dog, and he hunts like a jackal. Aziza – she's forgotten you, I'm sure. A prince's counsellor – her aim perhaps, achieved. And Mahnaz – there's thousands like her, with a project, looking for a spectre, you! – someone to promote....'

'I don't believe it, Tilda,' I say. 'I don't believe you know any of us.'

Yet – Tilda's is a fine intelligence. I ask, 'You're sure, Mahnaz hoped to be with me, make the trek to wisdom a companionship?'

'Of course,' she says. 'We're billiard balls, we kiss, think of our pockets, hit or miss ... But first – the orgy. Things will all seem cleaner when we've had some fun....'

*

'You aren't sick,' Tilda says. 'You don't need a mask. And if it's a disguise, since no one knows you – they might know your mask....'

She pulls me in: the room is large and full of guys in suits and frocks – here's a big dish, it's full of rusty keys. 'You're not a Palestinian,' Tilda says, pushing me along. 'You never had a home, so no one's stolen it. It's bad taste to put out that plate: forget the outside, Raul! Frisk and gambol! Here you're free, you're nothing but yourself – no house, no land, no history, no judgements and no politics....'

'It's an anomaly,' I say. 'Before you realised how all humans are the same, they put out this sort of dish, to have you swap around.... To change partners, you exchange car keys, and off you go with someone new....'

'No one's going anywhere,' says Tilda sharply. 'Not here. And we have just arrived. Why should we leave?'

'And neither of us has a car. Now, what do we do?' I ask.

'The music starts, you dance,' she says. 'And when it stops you take whatever you've been dancing with. If you're a Kirghiz – you hope it is a horse. As for you – take what's in front of you, so long as it's not me.... It won't be Mahnaz – she'll be in a hole, awaiting judgement or a test. She's fixated on the future, being there, existing in it, on her terms.... Beware desire and optimism ... they drive you with their spurs; no reins, no brakes ... no eyes....'

'But Tilda, you're my guide,' I say. 'Without you ... every moment's something different, without you, how'd I puzzle it all out?'

But Tilda's not a schoolman. If she knows, she tells; if not, she doesn't speculate. If I know, I mustn't tell – my friends have chosen the wrong sides, or are being punished, or are damaged – friendly fire or hostile: all the same, you musn't tell. That leaves the universe of an uncertainty that doesn't intrigue her – not at all....

'Look!' I say. 'There's lokumi – fifteen types....'

'How exactly,' Tilda asks. 'Do you have an orgy nowadays? I guess there are professionals – everybody looks much younger than their age, so there's no way to categorise ... it's hit or....'

There's angry people leaving contact rooms and cubicles. 'Perhaps you should come in parties,' I say. 'Or in threes and fours – maybe there's a floor show, a strip-tease....'

'You're prehistoric, Raul,' says Tilda.

'It must depend,' I say. 'I'm not sure what on. They say the Tsar is here....'

There's a tiny figure in white uniform – he looks Neapolitan, an ice-cream seller; a Selassie. He stands behind the buffet, like a part-time waiter – 'The tsarinas had to pull the waggons,' Tilda says, quite unimpressed, 'with all the stuff they'd gathered.'

No one knows us, we don't touch, as if we're all immaculate.

'I should talk to the Tsar,' I say. 'He's all alone....'

'Things will get better for him,' Tilda says. She has no pity, not for anyone, not herself. It's good: she goes on, 'He knows – life is about what happens: death. Nothing is cured, nothing's turned back, nothing's foreseen, foreseeable. Maybe I should have sex with him – those medals, though –

the ones you give yourself – it's rather infra dig of him, and so it would reflect on me. Although – sex is what you do to yourself, or else it's rape. It's complicated. Why did we come...?'

There's other angry people here – unsatisfied or disappointed – not purified, it seems.

'They say in heaven and in hell there is no sex,' says Tilda. 'If the tsars had read young Marx, they'd see when humankind is free, the time is spent without a thought of intercourse. For Rousseau, there's assemblies, for Freud the orgy was inside ... maybe it's Jung who gives a hint....'

There's scuffles and some shouting.

'Tilda, the idea's yours,' I say. 'Who organises tourneys like this anyway? Not ritual ... it's an industry. I saw a movie – "Folies de Pigalle" – it all seems low key and the actors ancient, snide. Maybe we forgot, you have to pay....'

'Someone!' Tilda shouts. 'Someone take control!'

A shout from somewhere, loud – 'Hurrah, hurrah – the Tsar, the Tsar!'

'I'm not for that,' I say to Tilda. 'No one hears you, Raul!' she says – another shout –

'The dance, the dance!' and the band plays – slow, a waltz. 'No, no,' shouts Tilda, breaking from my hold. 'Something with guts and teeth....'

'And beauty too,' the Tsar says, standing beside us, as I shrink away. 'Beauty, inventiveness ... the beat goes on....'

The crowd is round us, frocks agape and pants unzipped, they wait for his suggestion –

'The Rite of Spring,' the Tsar declares. 'Our own composer, our own tune.'

The band strikes up, nervous at first, tumTì, tumTì....

'Who'll be the sacrifice?' I ask, but no one hears – the orgiasts go quiet and listen with eyes closed, and bodies swaying, accelerating, jiggling a little to the rhythm, carried along 'how beautiful,' I hear, and then – 'A volunteer, a volunteer!'

'Maybe your time has come,' says Tilda, joshing me along – 'Enough of virgin maidens going to the chop: a fusty male – at last, at last ... the spring is here, and so's the sacrifice!'

'No, no!' I shout, my voice is muffled, but there's some who press up close to listen – 'Let's do it to the Tsar again!' – but Tilda says. 'No, no – history is done and cannot be done another time....'

There's doubt, confusion – the uncertainty ... supreme principle, as we know....

'You see,' says Tilda. 'If you'd gone and looked for Mahnaz – she would have used you, like she did before: it isn't love she offers, it's her plan.... To set you up, to change the world, and then – both feet on your shoulders, she's a tower of strength. You're on a slalom of bad luck, Raul, it's good. You take disasters like infections, to protect the rest of us.'

'I'd end like Lennox, the sequestered sage?' I ask.

Now, I remember the whole tale, the burrow in the sand, the impotence, the diet limited, begrudged ... the daily visits, quizzing; plagiarism too.... Lennox had reached a little wisdom, and it terrified. He had to dig....

'You seek Mahnaz,' says Tilda, 'and she seeks you. She leeches on.... If I were you, I'd take my overcoat, left at the door, leave a good tip, and run. That's all the wisdom you will get – it's very limited, but be content, it's the authentic thing....'

*

The music heats and throbs to climax: out comes the knife. It could be one they use to cut the nuptial cake, but where's the Bride? 'The Tsar, the Tsar!' – up goes the cry – 'Revenge! Down with the people – let him choose the victim, on it goes – the rite of vengeance – payback time!'

The Tsar is dithering, he holds the knife with dread, uncertainty – homicide? or suicide? Even a feminicide.... The history's on the teeter here: a camera crew runs in – Tilda's summoned them for sure, and 'Hold it!' someone says. 'Let them set up.... Lights, action...!'

*

'The Tsar – it's only dress-up,' Tilda says, and laughs and banters with the TV crew.

'There's a whole room of lookalikes, history in drag and fard,' she says. 'In dynasties, from places now gone arid, sour, but once were prosperous, with fairs and caravanserais ... the Ghorids and the Chingizids – done at school, forgotten now – and officials, soldiers, great powers they now call local and ephemeral – but with riches, horses, onagers, and ostriches galore....'

Her eyes show distance – how she engages with the lost and powerful – a procession through the studio, wise men and dolts, feminism and its militants, writers of dodge and stodge, deserters and heroes, lovers of nature, lovers of themselves....

'I'm sure there's wisdom here,' I say. 'But not in these....' as the replicants press round, the victims and the sacrifices, those who massacred, conscripted, starved, were starved....

'Oh, what a bore you are,' says Tilda. 'Your moralism! When it's done, it's done ... death, Raul. That is the purpose and the end, not hope and the new dawns. Dawn and dusk – a cycle inevitable, indifferent.... You need to show it. That's enough. The wise will understand, the stupid – weep.'

It's true. I tend to weep. I am not wise. Not yet.

'Stay, if you want, Raul,' says Tilda, changing register. 'Stay with me. We're used to each other.'

'But here,' I say, 'it's horror. These clowns who envy the dead, the pompous ... and the sacrifice, decided by that little bottle-stopper in the white sailor suit....'

'We're cats, Raul,' she says. 'We live, we die. We love to eat. When we couple, we scream. That – like everything – is over very quick. We like our bed, our chair, the fabrics and the smells, the place we crap and piss. A caress, a pirouette, our walk. We go wrong when we want more, or make a story. That is wisdom, Raul.... We watch. My life – is watching: the art of contemplation.'

*

Of course, I don't accept.

*

I go out in the street, no one stops me, no one bothers. If life is circular like they say, Mahnaz should be waiting for me. 'If the bus goes to the capital,' she'd say, 'we'll go together to the governor, tell him there's an uprising in view, but we can be of use to him – we have intelligence, or we could represent him over there, or maybe we'll represent the grievances, make him an offer.... Once inside their confidence, it's easy – they don't have ideas, don't know the street, don't trust their thugs.... We'll bend them....'

No Mahnaz. There's Khalil, though.

*

'You were with the Russians up there, Raul,' Khalil says.

'No, no Russians. All nationalities, indifferent. Just the music, Khalil,' I say. 'Horsing around – without a horse. Those guys feel they are in charge, but there's nothing original. History trudges round with sticky feet....'

'I find that too,' he says: 'Do you think it's good or bad? Why does originality bother you? Doing it right, the past – isn't that as good as trying something new?'

It's a sharp question. I think a while, and say: 'If what I was looking for was not unusual, out of the common drift, it wouldn't be worthwhile, I feel.'

'The expedition and the dig – they finished bad,' he says. 'And still the music draws you....'

As if what happened since was void, or an embellishment, an ornament, tied to a song.

It's a joke, not one that anyone would laugh at, though.

'I shouldn't want a choice. And yet – I do,' he says. 'Being a libertine, like when we two were good friends: or the monastic life....? When I knew you, I had no psychology ... no choices, right or wrong....'

'You want both lives?' I ask. 'A roué who's a monk – or turn and turn about?'

'In the monastery,' he says, 'everybody works at making life more comfortable for themselves, at cheating. It makes you want the real life, life outside. And then the libertine gets tired, and always bored. It's all banal....'

'I cannot hide you, Khalil,' I say. 'I've nowhere. At most, I'll hide myself, alone. A grave. Why do you seek me out?'

'When you're in a sect, a brotherhood, it's allies are the test,' he says. 'It's like the Bolsheviks. Those closest to you – are your enemies. The most unlikely – you think you can deal with them, you despise them, they're easy to deceive. They're your opposites – and so ... you take the risk, eliminate your brothers, love and trust your enemies. I'm running from my brothers....'

You don't ask – 'did you do awful things?' No soldier tells you anyway – that is their job. Loyalty, and killing people who have taken the wrong side, it isn't something you discuss.

He goes on, 'The philosophy remains, unchanged. Even more rigorous. But the cycles – these are short, lethal. Like the Mayan cities, every crisis lasting a few years – then recurring – and people leave. If they can't leave, they grow indifferent. It's not the long cycles: the short ones kill, they're unmanageable, they're devastating. You think in the same way as before, or think you do: but if you stay, stay faithful – you will die. You starve. You're abandoned – someone cuts you down.'

'But you were fighting, Khalil,' I say. 'A militant, opponent of regimes, at least.'

'It's different for us: we're not a civilisation, we're a fantasy,' he says. 'But history – it calls! You're in a city. Like Naachtun or Tikal. You're a body, with your kings and priests; if one dies, the whole, the body, starts to shake. The city is an organ, you're an organism with a single cell – vulnerable from many sides, but with a single pulse, life, destiny. The battles, the wars – those are short cycles – constant crises. You must be strong ... but inside you're hollow. The uncertainty ... wears you down. You sacrifice, you eat each other. There's victories and losses – it's all cycles, always mortality calls at your door, sometimes you open, sometimes not. It isn't up to you.'

'But the life – is different, the rules....' I say.

'Yes,' he says. 'The rules are different, totally. They're absolutely new – though it's the old ones polished up and painted. You have escaped from what and where you were. Your city is the centre of a world – the rest is alien – the people round about, don't follow your rules, know nothing of them. And you're tough, and indifferent to pain and suffering; an anthill, you and yours.'

'But here you are,' I say. 'Not an ant....'

'I don't know what I am,' he says. 'If I'm not with others like me, I have no picture of myself.'

'This, Khalil,' I say. 'It isn't wise. It's not a way to live.'

'You can live like this for centuries, Raul,' he says. 'You seek immortality, but it won't be so – the water runs out, there are tempests ... you don't make converts, you make slaves and prisoners. A terrible loneliness, ah! – the solitude ... of following the destiny – but all alone, thousands, millions of you.... Short lives lived intensely, but unloved.'

'I remember Fatimata,' I say, not knowing how to respond to him.

'That's why I'm here,' he says. 'I thought – I'll look up Raul, and start my life again, and see if I can take another route.

'Some evenings – she came when we weren't there – came and sang, and so and so and on and on until she'd had enough. Another way of life, hers, Raul ...Just – she quit. Ending when you want.... Doing your show, getting applause. Then – stop!'

'If you desert, you will be punished,' I say. 'We all desert, over and over – we get punished, quite arbitrarily – but you signed up.... You can break an oath, but never ever take it back....'

It's a puzzle, this wisdom. Desert – you're punished. Join something else, desert – you're punished. Everybody's punished – those who desert, and those who don't, this side or that....

*

'We should compare ourselves, each other's life, Khalil. Or maybe just: "you are my brother". Leave it there,' I say.

'I'm sure we each had principles, and some we shed, sometimes there were none, and other times we argued wrong,' he says.

'We come with nothing but our breath,' I say. 'And leave with even less. The rest – you should be very prudent: – for the individual, life counts. For history, for the species – what defines, is death.'

'My circumstances made me bad,' he says. 'Traditions, principles – made me worse....'

'It's hard not to have these creatures on your back,' I say. 'Then good and bad come in, not that they count for much unless you are divine, or a philosopher – you need to be a sage to parry and riposte....'

It's true, I think, but avoiding all your circumstances, emptying out and being pure – you end like Lennox, in the sand.

*

The orgy up above is ending, there's applause and shouts – 'onward' ... 'upward'. Tilda comes clattering down the steps – 'Aha!' says Khalil, holding on to her. 'I came for you! Let me tell my story, see if I am justified.... Camera and lights! You're my saviour, Tilda, you can expose me, pardon me....' His tongue skids, he's a confusion, he holds tight to her, she tries to force him off.

'You're Khalil?' Tilda says, between her apprehension and delight. 'You're a pariah. We give you a tribunal – you defend yourself, there is no judge....'

'I know,' he says. 'That is the void, the expanse of desolation – exposure. I'll walk with you, Tilda, you are my Cicero.... The valley of other people's deaths.... Under the lights, I'll tilt my face to you, I'll be your child, obey, ingratiate. Paint on a little colouring, to make me seem alive.'

'We'll see,' she says. 'Maybe we'll disguise you, to protect the rest....' She turns to me. 'You don't come out well, you know. If there are sides, a choice of what to do – you have no thoughts. All's left to free will: what you do, and what you don't, the judgements for yourself, and those you make for everybody else....'

'I didn't trust the Tsar....' I say.

'Oh, no one does,' she says. 'He doesn't ask for it – that's why he's Tsar!'

'And Tilda – did you make out with anyone?' I ask. I'm jealous, possessive, though I can't admit. 'Oh, with everyone,' she says. 'I'm quite carnivorous – forget the magic mushrooms; to dance with me, you don't need buy a ticket....' And she laughs.

THE EXPEDITION

'Start again,' says Khalil. 'You love expeditions, Raul – now, you and I.... Make it a tryst.'

I'm not enthusiastic. He's my brother, but, after all ... everybody is. He says, 'If God had made and loved us, he'd have left food out, ready-made, not have us starve and scavenge, eat sentient life, get sick. Then there's evolution, as if someone couldn't make up their mind....'

'I know,' I say. 'It used to bother everyone, but now the problem's been forked down, into the mulch of ordinary puzzlement....'

'There's money, too,' he says. 'What is it, where does it go? In your pants – they rob you. In the bank, it goes invisible ... it melts....'

'Dear Khalil,' I tell him, 'if we are to trek together – forget the questions of philosophy. Look at the landscape, read a map. Don't speculate. Decide – are we looking for a bird? A city? The garrulous, the local chatterers? Something invisible, hidden underground?'

We stand on the lakeshore. We have no bread – the birds, some swans, a goose, some little gulls ... scan us, reject, indifferent. 'The animals,' Khalil says. 'They mean no harm. But – we hassle them, we get diseased from them.'

There's a coypu ... escaped from a prison farm, quite clueless.... Wanting the home you cannot offer, can't imagine....

'Forget them,' Khalil says. 'They don't know if they are common, or they're rare. Who cares? Forget us diving too: it's like digging, but extreme.... Let's try something else entirely.'

'You're right,' I say. 'The animals – they make you love them. Your interest in them – unavailing and promiscuous. The baby flamingoes ... your massive first love, unrequited: and it dents your soul for ever....'

'It's useless, this burden on emotions, always heavier,' Khalil says. 'I understand why people don't bother with what's round and over them, unless it's worth a buck. The ruins, those fragile skeletons that once were roaring beasts ...

it's over, the revealing, the immortalising them.... That's over, it will pass, the logic isn't on their side. Life! Long live! Forget the animals: life is your sphere, the rest is separate and alien.'

Tilda says, 'Decide, Khalil. Both of you – your lives are tortuous and unconfessable. I watch you, and explorers like you – the blustering, concealment, and uncertainty. I see it all – but I can't move in front of you, can't lead – can only show how much I know, how much I must depend on you.... I am the eye of truth – I'll follow you and be discrete, but peek continually....'

*

'Come, Khalil,' I say. 'If we wait here, we'll never leave – though there's no conclusion either way. We should be off. The songs agree. If Tilda wants to follow us – it's painless, there's no complication there....'

'She's a fine woman,' Khalil says. 'Tilda. Gives the orders, but keeps away from consequences.... Has a robust frame to hang her baubles on. It's to her credit, her sensibility. She had a dog once, now she won't have another one. That is a tribute....'

'When we're on the road, Khalil,' I say. 'We might need pills – for inspiration, and if there is no food....'

'That's fine,' he says. 'We lived on pills. All soldiers do.'

'Talking of people we might meet,' I say, 'the one we should avoid – is my interrogator, Sami – a beetle of a man, he couldn't lift you off the ground and on the hook. But he gives orders that's obeyed. The only redeeming point – his daughter lost a leg, out on her bicycle....'

'Some parents are too indulgent with their kids,' he says. 'But losing a leg is careless....'

And we laugh.

Think of the music. Of Fatimata, not of Khalil; of what he might have done; whether my fears of him are justified or paranoid, and marvel – how it's all run off him, his skin quite waterproof....

'Since you don't ask,' he says, 'and all your mates are dead and buried in their hole: your Lamya, who you don't reflect upon – she finished bad. Spied for the police, then when that stopped – the neighbours wouldn't speak to her ... her kids....'

I push the talk away from her, on to Aziza. 'Too bad, Khalil, you'll never taste her biscuits – and her herbal teas.... She still holds a salon, I'll bet, every politico who aspires will pass through there. And Mahnaz – maybe she'll go through Aziza's ritual – political succession.... As you know, it's hopeless in those straightened lands, where despot follows despot – each one propelled by hopes.'

'Aziza was plump – fortunately for her, she had a big divan to spread out on.... And tiny Mahnaz, looking for her saviour, a father for her people, not that they reciprocated – let's hope she isn't sat upon....'

We laugh again. No doubt, we're tense.

'Your military skills, Khalil,' I say. 'I depend on you; don't use those rough tricks on me!'

I laugh, to show I'm cool about his past, whatever that might be: 'Inspiration,' I say. 'That's the word. That's what we must seek. Tilda follows us, she's smart, she'll recognise it if we find a treasure....'

'That is the goal,' Khalil agrees. 'But – that's the start as well ... the treasure's us....'

'Of course,' I say. 'You'd be content, Khalil, with inspiration – the afflatus. Me ... I want the further stage.

'I seek wisdom.

'If it's not found, should we then say, "That is the limit, anything more is up to me!"... The challenge, Khalil....

'The search. Wisdom. Wear stout shoes, Khalil, and cut a stave.... Much of our route will take us upward, up towards the peaks that we see distant, perching expectant in a swirl of cloud and mist.'

1

About the author

John Fraser has lived in Rome since 1980. Previously, he worked in England and Canada.

www.ingramcontent.com/pod-product-compliance
Lightning Source LLC
Chambersburg PA
CBHW020551310726
48979CB00008B/1173/J

* 9 7 8 1 9 1 0 3 0 1 8 7 6 *